TEACHER'S DEAD

BENJAMIN ZEPHANIAH

BLOOMSBURY

LONDON OXFORD NEW YORK NEW DELHI SYDNEY

BY THE SAME AUTHOR

Face
Refugee Boy
Gangsta Rap

Bloomsbury Publishing, London, Oxford, New York, New Delhi and Sydney

First published in Great Britain in September 2007 by Bloomsbury Publishing Plc
50 Bedford Square, London WC1B 3DP

This paperback edition published in January 2018

www.bloomsbury.com

BLOOMSBURY is a registered trademark of Bloomsbury Publishing Plc

A CIP catalogue record for this book is available from the British Library

ISBN 978 1 4088 9501 6

MIX
Paper from
responsible sources
FSC® C020471

Typeset by Newgen Knowledge Works Pvt. Ltd., Chennai, India
Printed and bound in Great Britain by CPI Group (UK) Ltd, Croydon CR0 4YY

1 3 5 7 9 10 8 6 4 2

For the truth, and the
seekers of truth

CHAPTER 1

The Ending

The knife was pushed so far into Mr Joseph's stomach that it almost came out of his back. Lionel Ferrier closed his eyes, held the handle tight, and turned it vigorously. Mr Joseph grunted towards the sky as the knife was twisted deep into his intestines, and as the sharp stainless steel sliced through his organs blood pumped out of his body with so much force that it splattered Lionel's chest. Lionel pulled the knife out and jogged away slowly with his friend Ramzi Sanchin following behind him.

They weren't hiding their faces as they ran, and they weren't running to avoid being caught, they were just going somewhere else. The attack took place in front of dozens of other pupils, who looked on horrified, many of them screaming, and all of them too scared to go to their teacher's rescue.

'Don't just stand there!' screamed head boy Otis. 'Get some help, go and get some help!'

His hands trembled so much that it took him several attempts to turn on his mobile phone; as soon as it was on he called the police, who arrived ten minutes later. But it was too late; Mr Edgar Arnold Joseph had already drawn his last breath in the arms of Otis Westwood the head boy and Mrs Cartwright the history teacher.

CHAPTER 2

The Crime Scene

My name is Jackson Jones. I stood and watched a teacher die. For the first time in my life I felt real shock. I didn't panic, I just froze. I wanted to walk away but I couldn't. I tried to walk towards the place of death but I couldn't. I was the quickest at the one hundred metres in my year, I had only been beaten once in the long jump, and my reflexes were sharp, but all that stuff was useless. My whole body actually went numb. They say the brain is like a computer – well, my computer crashed.

Lionel and Ramzi were the same age as me. I knew Lionel, we were friends once, for a short while. Actually we were only friends for two days until we fell out over my MP3 player. I lent it to him and when I got it back it was broken, the screen was damaged. I'd say hello to him sometimes but we were never close friends. I didn't hate him for it, I just didn't trust him. I didn't know Ramzi much, I hardly ever spoke to him, but there was something about him. I didn't trust him either.

I will never forget the way Lionel put that knife into Mr Joseph. He was so calm, and he did it with such ease. As I watched them both jogging away I thought they must have done this before. They were like hardened gangsters in a movie. It was like just another day at the office, and nobody dared try to go after them.

Films brainwash you. When people die in films the way the blood trickles down the shirt can look quite cool, the death is usually accompanied by music, and they always have just enough time to deliver their last lines, usually a message for the woman or man they love, or their mother, or a message for the whole of mankind. The way Mr Joseph went down was nothing like that. First there was the force of the blood, then urination, and then the very violent convulsions, and the desperate gasping for breath as his body tried to hold on to life. I knew exactly when his body gave up the fight: there was a moment of silence, his back arched, his body stiffened, and then he took his last breath. Trust me, it was nothing like in the movies.

The school was surrounded by police, all entrances were sealed off with that flimsy tape that they always use, and an ambulance came and put a curtain around the body before taking it away. Those of us who saw what happened were told to line up in the dining hall and wait for our parents to come so that we could be questioned by the police. Although I was hungry I didn't mind waiting, but I felt guilty for feeling hungry, after all this was much more important than my food. I should have been feeling sick after what I just saw, but I was thinking of food.

I looked out of the dining-hall window and saw my mother talking to a newspaper reporter. The reporter gave her a business card and she pushed her way to the front of the crowd and identified herself to the police who were guarding the school gate. As soon as my mother saw me she raced towards me. She's small, but she's strong, and when she put her arm around me and squeezed me she almost took my voice away. I could feel the relief in her voice.

'Jackson, are you all right?'

'Yes, Mum, I'm all right.' I groaned into the collar of her coat.

She stepped back to look at me. 'Are you hurt?'

'No, Mum, but Mr Joseph's been killed. Lionel Ferrier stabbed him, I saw it. None of us kids were attacked, but that Lionel, he just stabbed Mr Joseph and went off. I saw it with my own eyes, I was right near.'

CHAPTER 3

Boy A and Boy B

I was expecting something like an interrogation. Maybe television is to blame again, but I really thought that after witnessing a murder I would be subjected to hours of heavy questioning in a dark room, but all they did that day in the hall was ask me what I saw, and all I did was tell them what I saw. After speaking to other pupils I learnt that it was the same for all the witnesses. Then that thing happened, that thing when a group of people watch the same incident but see different things. Apparently it's because of the shock and the stress, and the excitement, if you can call it that. We were also offered counselling but no one accepted the offer, or no one admitted to it, even though we were warned that the effects of what we all witnessed may not be felt until much later. There was lots of crying, especially from the girls. Some boys too, but mainly girls. To be really honest, I felt like crying but I didn't. To be really, really honest, I shed a tear or two, but I was silent, and because I was silent I don't think it can really be called crying. Whatever.

Watching someone die is not easy, I don't care what kind of front people put up. I put up a front, I had to, I'm a boy, but deep down I was feeling it. It wasn't too bad when I was busy doing things, but it would get to me when I stopped, or when I was just about to sleep, or just after I woke up. But I never cried, not really. Sometimes I would see the whole thing happening again in my mind. When that happened I just told myself that this was the real world, and if this was the real world I should be prepared to see more acts of violence, more death, and more destruction.

After Lionel stabbed Mr Joseph he jogged to the park with Ramzi, put his shirt in a rubbish bin, cleaned the blood off the knife, and then he and Ramzi both lit cigarettes. When the police arrived they were sitting on the park bench puffing away and saying nothing. The police were surprised to see how relaxed the boys were. Lionel still had the knife in his hand, an officer took it, and without the slightest hint of resistance they both walked to the police car surrounded by officers. The newspapers picked up on this. Boy A and Boy B, as they were called, were being described as 'Teen Killers', 'Blood Brothers', and 'The Unteachables'. They were being compared to other young killers, and many so-called experts were coming up with hundreds of so-called character profiles.

Radio phone-in programmes were swamped with people calling in with their opinions. Most of the callers were falling into two camps. Some were complaining that it was the fault of television and that if we kept allowing our children to get out of control we would end up like America. Others were saying the only way to stop them is to execute them like they do in America.

The school was closed down for a week, and every day more and more flowers were being placed on the railings. The Queen sent a message and spelt the school name wrong, the Prime Minister sent us a message saying how proud he was of the way we all handled a time of great difficulty, but a month before he had been on television calling us a failed school, threatening to close us down or send in a 'super head teacher'. Suddenly kids who hated writing started to write short poems and place them with the flowers. A policewoman was given the job of making sure that all those who came to pay their respects were able to, and that all the flowers were properly placed and could be seen.

Lionel and Ramzi were taken to court the day after the killing and remanded in youth custody. The court ordered that reports were made ready for the hearing. The media made a big deal out of the fact that both boys were accompanied only by their mothers. 'Fatherless Killers' one newspaper called them. I wasn't going to judge them for that. I had never seen my father, I didn't even know who he was, but that didn't make me evil. I'd been alive for fifteen years and I'd never felt the need to kill someone because I didn't have a dad.

Back then I used to listen to a lot of music, mainly dance bands like The Chemical Brothers, and hip-hop bands like Positive Negatives, I used to go for all types of British bands. Then all this happened. I kept listening to music, but I became more interested in the lyrics. I suppose I was looking for the meaning of life but I soon realised I weren't going to find that out from a singer who was a spotty teenager like me. I also started looking a lot – I mean really looking. I would stare at people and wonder if they were capable of killing someone. I even started looking at myself in the mirror and asking the same question. Could I?

CHAPTER 4

A Mourning of Celebration

The first time I saw Mrs Joseph I couldn't take my eyes off her. She came to school to speak in the morning assembly. It was two weeks after the death of her husband and the school was still in mourning. As we sat through the head teacher's speech I watched Mrs Joseph. I could not stop my eyes coming back to her, and when I was looking at her the head teacher's speech just became background noise. I could only see Mrs Joseph; everything else in my field of vision became a blur. As I stared at her I realised that there were so many questions in my mind that needed to be answered. I knew how I felt having seen her husband die, but I began wondering what it was like for her to suddenly find that her husband wasn't there.

When Mrs Martel, the head teacher, invited her on to the stage you could feel the anticipation in the hall. This was going to be heavy. Some kids held their heads down, about five pupils began to clap their hands, but when they realised that they were in the minority they stopped. Mrs Joseph surprised us all.

She smiled as she took to the stage and started her speech by telling us not to feel sorry for her. She walked to and fro across the stage, unlike Mrs Martel, who always stood still when speaking.

'I think it would be hard for anyone to imagine the pain that I've been through,' she said on the move. 'My husband kissed me goodbye one morning, and came to this wonderful school, to do what he loved doing best, teaching you wonderful kids. He even called me at lunchtime and told me that he was having a really good day. He told me that one pupil had come up to him and said, "Sir, you rock," which apparently meant that he was good. The moment I was told of his death I didn't believe it. After all I had just spoken to him and he had said he was having a good day. And anyway he was at school – teachers get killed in American schools, I thought, not in our great British schools. But I soon couldn't hide from the reality. For many days I locked myself away, I kept my house in darkness and I communicated with the world outside as little as I possibly could. There was a numbness of all my senses. When I touched things they didn't feel the same. I could no longer hear the simple sounds that I normally found pleasure in, like birds singing in my garden, or snatches of conversation from people walking past my house. The only comfort I really found was in the darkness. Then I began to feel angry, I mean really angry. I turned into this person that I didn't like. I never lose my temper, but now I found myself smashing things, some things that I really valued. I became aggressive and bitter, and then I started feeling sorry for myself.

'But soon I realised how much that was holding me back. I had lost my husband, the man I loved, but the more I kept feeling sorry for myself the more depressed I got. I remember just after we got married, Edgar, or Mr Joseph as you know him, lost his mother in a car crash. I hardly knew his mother, but I was so saddened by this sudden death that I found it difficult to eat and do everyday things, but he told me that his mother wouldn't want us to wallow in sadness. He said that his mother would want us to take stock of what had happened and move on. He gave me a lecture on the difference between mourning a death and celebrating a life. Edgar's mother turned him into a celebrator of life, Edgar turned me into a celebrator of life, and I want you to celebrate his life.

'There are still many questions to be answered, but I have stopped asking, why me? I am moving on. I have to. I don't know how much you realise this, but Edgar loved teaching, and he loved teaching you. Some of the knowledge you have is a little bit of Edgar that lives on in you. I want you to celebrate his life; I want each one of you to live on. Thank you.'

Not once did I take my eyes off her. I had heard that celebration of life thing before but it usually came from a priest, or a teacher. It seemed like an easy thing to say, but I found it astonishing this time because it was Mr Joseph's wife who was speaking. She had less anger, and less sorrow, than any one of us in that hall on that morning.

When the assembly was over I managed to get close to Mrs Joseph. I was nervous but I had to ask her a question.

'Excuse me, Mrs Joseph. I'm sorry if you think I'm being rude, but I just wanted to know. Don't you feel like you want revenge or something? OK, maybe not revenge, but justice, don't you want justice?'

She smiled. 'Justice? What is real justice? That's not my main concern. I want to use this time to think, to think about life, death, and everything else that we have to do with our time. I want to think about moving forward, I have thoughts about life without my husband, but I also spare some thoughts for the parents of whoever killed my husband.'

'What do you think about them?' I asked.

She wasn't sure who I meant. 'The killers or the parents?'

'The parents,' I said.

'Well, I think that they never killed him, and I just wonder what they are going through.'

'Do you know them?'

'No,' she replied. 'But I know that they are humans, whoever they are.'

A voice came from behind me. 'Move on now, Jones.' It was Mrs Martel. 'I don't want to rush you, but you do have a lesson to go to.'

That's when I started thinking, that's when I started asking questions. Why was it that the people causing trouble in the media were the people who were most removed from the situation? Could Mrs Joseph, the person closest to the victim, really be so forgiving? I wanted to know what kind of fifteen-year-old goes to school with a knife and kills his teacher. I knew that Lionel had had arguments with Mr Joseph, but so had I. I knew some people thought Lionel was a bit weird, but lots of people thought I was weird too. I knew that some people said he was dangerous, but what did that mean? They also said Neil Franks was dangerous because he was a wicked MC, and swallowing chewing gum was dangerous because it would stick to your heart, and kissing was dangerous because you could get cold sores. So dangerous meant many things. Were people scared of danger, or were people scared of the truth?

CHAPTER 5

A Small Tree Planted

When I first heard about the way Mr Joseph was buried I thought it was really weird. The only people there were his wife and a small group of relatives. The press were asked to stay away and all Mrs Joseph asked of the school was that we send our thoughts. She didn't mean write them down and send them by post, she meant that we should just think them, the idea being that they would arrive under their own steam. What I thought was even weirder was where he was buried. He was buried in some woodland, in a biodegradable cardboard coffin, with no flowers and no gravestone, just a small tree planted where a gravestone would have been. At first I thought it was all a bit nutty but then I began to understand. He wasn't religious, so there was no priest, just a friend talking about him and reading some of his favourite poems. Compare that to what we did at school.

Our head teacher organised a big memorial service. Other local schools were invited, as were the families of all the pupils, the local bishop, imam and rabbi, and a pagan, and a Hindu priest, and the world's media were there to record it all. My mother didn't make it, she said she wanted to, but she just couldn't afford to take a day off work. Still, there were so many people there that they even put speakers out in the playground for everyone who had to stand outside. The great and the good all stood up and did their speeches but they all sounded as if they weren't speaking to us in the hall, they sounded like they were speaking to the TV cameras, all doing mini performances, all except Mrs Joseph. What she said was pretty much what she'd said in the assembly some weeks before but she still sounded like she was speaking to us, she was still very personal, and because it was so real she was the only one who didn't get applause after her speech. Everyone was stunned into silence.

After the service everyone flocked around Mrs Joseph, and outside the school she was stopped by people with microphones desperately seeking something for the six o'clock news. I really wanted to speak to her again but I knew I stood no chance whilst the television people surrounded her. Fortunately as soon as they got what they wanted they were off. All I had to do now was get past Mrs Martel, who had become her private bodyguard. That was tough. I had to wait until almost everyone had gone before I could make my move, and then they were heading for the staffroom and I knew that if they went in there I would have to wait ages before she came out. So I made my move, and just as I was making my move I realised that I didn't have anything to say.

'Hello, Mrs Joseph. Good to see you again. Well, not good really, if you know what I mean. I mean, it's good to see you, but not like this. I mean, sorry.'

'Don't be sorry,' she said. 'I know what you mean. Sometimes I say things that just don't come out right. Don't worry, I know what you're trying to say.' She paused for a moment before adding, 'I remember you. We met before.'

'That's right,' I said, happy to be remembered. 'When you spoke at the assembly.'

Mrs Martel interrupted. 'He's always asking questions, this one.'

'That's not a bad thing,' said Mrs Joseph.

'I suppose you have a question ready right now,' said Mrs Martel.

'Yes I do,' I said quickly. As I replied I realised that once again I didn't have anything to say. But I had to say something.

'Are you OK?' I said finally.

'I'm OK,' Mrs Joseph replied.

Mrs Martel looked at me, rather puzzled. 'Are you OK?'

'Yes, I'm fine.'

I could see that Mrs Martel was about to dismiss

me. She spoke to me as if she was in class.

'Well, what do you have to say?'

So I said the first thing that came into my mind.

'My name is Jackson Jones. I'm one of the witnesses.'

Mrs Joseph reached out and shook my hand. 'Pleased to meet you, Jackson. How are you coping?'

'I'm doing OK.'

'The students have all been offered counselling,' said Mrs Martel.

'Is it helping?' asked Mrs Joseph.

'Well,' I hesitated. 'I'm not actually having any counselling, but you could say I'm having a kind of therapy.'

'I didn't know that,' said Mrs Martel.

'Interesting,' said Mrs Joseph.

'It's therapy that's like individually tailored to me. Maybe I'll tell you about it another time.'

Mrs Joseph smiled. 'Yes.'

'OK, Jackson. On your way now,' said Mrs Martel. 'He's a strange one. Harmless, but strange.'

That's Mrs Martel, our great head teacher. She would often speak about you as if you weren't there. There was absolutely no subtlety about her. When I told her that I was having a kind of therapy tailored to me she just presumed I was paying someone money to talk to them. She couldn't imagine that I was finding my own way of dealing with it, and I was. I was traumatised by what I saw, and I was pretty sure it was going to stay with me for the rest of my life, but we all have different ways of overcoming things, and my way is to try to understand why things happen. I just didn't want to lie back and let life happen to me. My mother said that when I was small the word I said the most was *why*. But I wasn't going to tell Mrs Martel all that so, 'Goodbye,' I said. And I went home.

CHAPTER 6

Between the Lines

That evening my mother brought home a whole stack of newspapers, much more than usual. I watched her as she flicked through the pages, stopping briefly every now and again, but then carrying on after a quick scan.

'Mum, what are you up to?'

'A friend at work said she saw you in a paper,' she said, excited. Then she yelled, 'There you are. Look at the state of you, you don't half look miserable.'

'Mum, it was a memorial service, not a graduation ceremony.'

'Yes, but it's not the end of the world.'

'No, Mum, it's not the end of the world, but it's the end of someone's life.'

Mum read quietly for a moment before adding, 'Well, it says here that Mrs Joseph said that the service is not about someone dying, but about someone living. She said it's a celebration of life, so there.'

'I know, and I agree with her, but I still think it's no time for fun and games, you have to be respectful.'

My mum knew I was right but she had to have the last word.

'All I'm saying is looking like you hate yourself is not being respectful.'

But I wouldn't let her have the last word.

'And all I'm saying is, it's not about the way you look, it's about the way you feel.' I reached out for the newspaper. 'Let me have a look.'

It has to be said, I did look really sad, but I didn't remember feeling that sad. I came to the sad conclusion that this was how I looked when I wasn't wearing any particular expression. It was my default face.

Mum left the room and I went and sat on the floor where the rest of the newspapers were and began to scan through them myself. Every one of them covered the memorial service, and every one of them claimed to be an exclusive. Then a report caught my eye. It was by Mark Townsend, a local journalist who had gone on to the local streets to ask people what they thought should happen to Boy A and Boy B. The piece had the headline, 'Let them bleed'. The worst quote of all came from a boy called Adi Macenzi. He said, 'Those two are children of the devil, and they should go to hell and burn in everlasting fire, like their father, the devil.'

It wasn't just that I thought it was a terrible thing to say, which I thought it was, what really got me was the person who was saying it. Adi Macenzi had left school earlier that year but before he left he made sure he earned himself the reputation as the worst bully ever in the history of school. With his back-up of four followers he would demand sweets, goods and money, with menaces. For the last three months before he left he made my life hell, and he drove Delbert Singh to attempt suicide. Delbert left and moved on to another school, but Adi Macenzi got away free. He wasn't even approached about it. Apparently there was no evidence. There may not have been any evidence but every pupil in school knew the truth and most were just too scared to say. I was. I knew about the school's no-bullying policy, it was pasted all over the walls. I knew that if you let bullies get away with it they got away with it more, but he was smart enough not to get caught by teachers, and we were all scared. No one was willing to make the first move to end his reign of terror. We all thought that if we did one of his cronies would step up and take his place. When he did leave school one of his cronies did take his place, Terry Stock, another vicious waste of space. I knew now that I had to talk to Adi Macenzi. Sitting in front of a counsellor wasn't my style but understanding what happened was, it would be my therapy.

I knew that Macenzi spent his days hanging outside a train station selling on used tickets. His nights were spent outside a local club trying to get clubbers to use illegal taxis, so it wasn't difficult finding him. On my first visit to the train station that Saturday afternoon I found him trying to convince two Polish students that buying a couple of return tickets from him would be cheaper than buying them over the counter because of something to do with peak times. Fortunately they realised that there were no peak times on Saturdays and they walked away. Macenzi turned and bumped into me.

'Jackson Jones, my old friend, what can I do for you, or what can I do you for? You know I like to do you.'

He hadn't changed one bit, but I had.

'I suggest you start doing something for yourself,' I said.

'Tough talk, be careful or you may get a slap. I think you may need a slap,' he said, stepping towards me.

'I think you may need a job,' I said, standing firm.

He laughed loud enough for his friends who were also dealing dirty tickets to notice.

'You're growing up quickly, Mr Jones.'

'I've just come to ask you something.'

'Ask away, Mr Jones.'

A couple of his friends came and stood next to him but I just wasn't in the mood to be intimidated.

'I saw you in the newspaper this week.'

'The press are all over me, I know. Fame, I'm coming to terms with it,' he said, looking to his friends, who smiled on cue.

'Well,' I continued. 'Who are you to say that whoever killed Mr Joseph should burn in hell? Look at all the stuff that you've done.'

He laughed even louder. 'Are you mad? I don't like teachers but at least I've never tried to kill one.'

'So you think bullying and driving people towards suicide is a good thing?'

'What you talking about, boy?' he said, moving another step towards me. 'The only thing I did was run a protection business. You know me, I've always been a business man, and if you read the news and listen to the politician people they're all trying to encourage small business people like me. Yeah, boy, I'm an entrepreneur. The police, they do protection, I was just running a private protection business.'

I kept standing my ground.

'I can guarantee you no one ever felt protected by you, and yes, I can see by what you're doing here that you're a business man.'

'You're getting so brave. I still say I never killed anyone, and never mind saying whoever killed Mr Joseph, it wasn't whoever who killed him, it was Lionel Ferrier who killed him. You know it, I know it, and by the time I'm done everyone will know it. He's a weirdo, his mum's a weirdo, and his friend's a

24

weirdo. Just ask anyone on Fentham Road and they'll tell you.'

'And what happens on Fentham Road?' I asked.

'That's where he lived. You don't know anything, do you?'

'I may not know a lot, but at least I'm not a bully,' I said, looking for a way out.

His two friends began to walk around the back of me, and he moved even closer.

'At least I believe in God, so yeah, they should burn in hell. Now go before I slap you,' he said, clenching his teeth.

I didn't have the energy to argue with him, and suddenly I wasn't feeling so brave.

'Of course,' I said. 'I'll go before you slap me, and you just keep believing in God.'

CHAPTER 7

A Place of Safety

I decided to go to Fentham Road that evening. It was a road I had passed many times before but one that I had never been down. It was the kind of road that didn't really lead anywhere, so if you didn't have any reason for going there you wouldn't. I got there at seven o'clock and children were playing football across the street, dogs seemed to be barking in every house in competition with the music, which seemed to be coming from every house. I also noticed that an unusually high number of men were working on their cars. The street was like a dog sanctuary, cum playground, cum car workshop, cum carnival. I know what this is, I thought, it's a tight-knit community. How nice, I thought, until I was approached by a boy around my age dressed in denims that were so big he looked like he was hiding another person in them.

'Not from round these ends, are you?'

'Not really,' I replied.

There was an empty plastic bottle on the floor; he kicked it towards me.

'What do you mean, not really? You're either from these ends or you're not. Are you from central or what?'

'No I'm not from central.'

'So where you from?'

'Why do you want to know?'

'Just talk when I talk to you.'

'I told you,' I said as convincingly as I could. 'I'm not from central.'

'I doesn't matter anyway, just go before I blow.'

Of course I felt it very unfair that he should speak to me that way, but I realised as I replied that I was beginning to sound like my head teacher.

'How dare you speak to me like that? I have the right to walk down this street.'

Suddenly he shouted out loud, 'Tommer, Craig, Fudge, come here. There's a kid here thinks he's got the right to walk down this street.'

He called three, but six appeared. I decided to use the best self-defence move I knew – I turned and I ran. But as I began to run I was stopped by four more who were waiting behind me, the most frightening of them being two girls.

One of the boys shouted, 'Let me do him.'

Another of the girls shouted, 'No, it's my turn.'

And a woman's voice from nowhere shouted, 'Leave him alone, what's he done to you?'

I liked the sound of that voice but as she argued

with the small boy in the big clothes I just couldn't see where it was coming from. The boy shouted at her as he continued to look my way.

'Why don't you shut your big mouth?'

She shouted, 'Have some manners.' I saw her leaning out of an upstairs window a couple of houses down from where I was standing.

'Up yours,' the boy shouted back.

Then a man appeared next to the woman in the window.

'Hey, you, don't talk to my missus like that.'

The boy replied defiantly, 'I'll talk to her how I want.'

'No you won't. I'll come down and make sure of that,' he said, leaving the window.

'Run for it, lads,' the boy shouted. And in a moment they had all scattered.

By the time the man got down I was standing there alone. I was beginning to see him as a bit of a hero until he spoke.

'What are you doing around here anyway? We're sick of people like you coming around here and starting trouble.'

Not sure what to say I said, 'Thanks.'

'Don't thank me,' he said, looking down at me as if he hated my guts. 'I didn't do anything to earn your thanks. Just think yourself lucky. Go, cos if you don't they'll come back and tear you apart, or they'll get their dogs to do it for them. Now change your location.'

The woman, who was obviously his missus, turned up.

'Leave him alone, Jason. He's had enough as it is, he must be freaked out. He's not from round here.'

I wasn't very good at reading faces on this day. She looked at me like she wanted to kill me and said, 'Do you want to come in? Fancy a cup of tea?'

I was surprised. Her man wasn't.

'Do you have to invite every Tom, Dick and Harry in? What's wrong with you? Is my company not good enough for you?'

'Meaning?' she said, placing her hands on her hips.

'Meaning nothing,' he said as he walked back into the house.

She looked me up and down as if she was thinking of adopting me.

'What's your name, son?'

'Jackson.'

'Yeah, OK. Jackson. What's your first name?'

'That is my first name.'

'Jackson, really? Don't tell me your second name's Jackson as well. Jackson Jackson, is it?'

'No. My name is Jackson Jones.'

'Jackson Jones. I like it.'

Another woman was negotiating her way past us on the pavement. As she passed she said, 'He's a bit young for you, isn't he, Carla?'

'He'll grow up,' she replied.

Even the nice people around here are really frightening, I thought.

'So is your name Carla?' I asked.

'Let's say I answer to that name when I'm in a good mood. Now come on in before we end up in the papers.'

On entering the hall I was confronted by shoes that looked as if they were trying to escape. The living room was packed with furniture; it was difficult to see the floor. I made myself small and squeezed around a large wooden coffee table in the centre of the room and sat down on a settee. There wasn't much room for sitting; like the other chairs in the room it was covered with cushions.

'That's right. Sit down and make yourself comfortable, I'll go and make you a cup of tea. How do you like your tea?'

'With one sugar,' I said.

She lifted her head towards the ceiling and shouted at the top of her voice, 'Jason, do you want a cup a tea?'

'No,' he shouted back. 'Bring me a beer from the fridge.'

'OK,' she replied as she turned back to me. 'Hey, you don't want a beer as well, do you?

I shook my head.

'He lives here but I never see him,' she continued. 'He's fixing our wardrobe now, he'll be in the loft tomorrow, the garden shed the day after, then he'll break the wardrobe again so that he can fix that again. Anything to avoid talking to me.'

She left, leaving me staring into a blank television screen that was so big I couldn't help watching it even though nothing was on. She soon came back with the tea. The tea tasted as if it had five sugars in it, or maybe one very big teaspoon. It was so sweet that when I tasted it I wanted to spit it out, but after all the effort she had made I thought I should at least act grateful.

'Thanks. Great,' I lied.

'Everyone loves my cuppas,' she said proudly.

'I can see why,' I lied again.

She sat down at the other side of the room next to television.

'So where are you from, then?'

'Why does everyone around here want to know where I'm from? Is it that important?'

Carla took a cushion and hugged it against her stomach. 'The thing is, people around here want to know everything. Not just where you're from, they want to know everything, and if you're a stranger you stand out. Everyone round here knows each other. But not me. No, I mind my own business. Don't go putting your nose in other people's business, that's what I say. Keep myself to myself, that's what I do.'

'Do you have any kids?' I asked.

'Yeah. Two girls. One's your age, and one's a bit younger. They're out now. So tell me, Jackson, what school do you go to?'

'Marston Hall.'

'Oh, you go to Marston, do you?' she said, dragging her words. 'They're in the news a lot lately.'

I played ignorant. 'You mean about the government calling us useless?'

'No, you know, the murder. Terrible thing. Those two boys, you know, the papers call them A and B, but down here we know who they are. One of them lives on this road, Lionel his name is. Strange one, him.'

I nodded my head slowly to give the impression that I was thinking.

'Oh yes. Yes. I know what you're talking about. So what's so strange about him?' It was as if she was waiting for me to ask.

'Well, he acts like he's on another planet. He's fifteen years old and still sucking his thumb, he's in and out of that house at all times of the night, he's always got his head down in the gutter, and when he raises his chin he looks like death warmed up. I mean, he's so miserable. He grew up around here all his life but he's never played with the local boys, he never speaks to the girls, he just never mixes with anyone. And he smells funny, and he's always in the same clothes, and if you say hello to him all he says back is, hello.'

She left a space for me to speak.

'What do you want him to say?'

'I don't know, he should say something. Not just hello. What? Don't they teach you conversational skills at that school?'

Jason appeared at the door with a large screwdriver in his hand.

'Why don't you go and teach them some of your so-called conversational skills. You could speak for England, you, no, Europe, you could speak for Europe.'

'I'm just telling him about that killer boy Lionel.'

'You should mind your own business,' he said, pointing the screwdriver towards her and continuing his rant. 'Just leave people's business. He'll get his comeuppance, the dirty little lowlife scum. Fancy taking a knife to school and killing a teacher. I know what I'd do if he was my son. They wouldn't need to lock him up; I'd deal with the little toe rag myself. But he hasn't got a father, has he? No, he's got an absentee father, that's what he's got. Lowlife scum, that's what he is. And his mother, they should lock her up too. Any chance of a bite to eat, love?'

Carla stood up and threw the cushion back on to the seat. 'Do you want something to eat, son?'

She was talking to me more and more like an adopted son. A bit worrying, I thought.

'No,' I said, standing up. 'I have to go now. Thanks for everything, and thanks for saving me from the mob. I've had to face two mobs today. Will I be all right out there now?'

'Yes. Just turn right and keep walking. Come back sometime. You're always welcome. Best tea on the street.'

Just as I was leaving the house her two daughters turned up. They walked past me in the doorway as if I wasn't there.

Carla noticed. 'Rachel, Pauline, this is Jackson. Say hello.'

They stopped, turned, and said, 'Hello, Jackson' in unison, and then they continued to head towards the kitchen.

'Goodbye, Jackson,' said Carla, shaking her head. 'They're in a bad mood, they always come home in a bad mood after they visit their father.'

CHAPTER 8

A Trip to Trinidad

Carla said I would be all right when I left the house, that I should turn right and keep walking. I turned right and I had to run for my life. But I didn't hold it against her; she wasn't to know that the local kids were waiting for me to finish my tea.

In the school assembly on Monday morning Mrs Martel gave us a lecture on the virtues of forgiveness. Using quotes from Jesus, the Buddha, Mahatma Ghandi and John Lennon, she told us that the inability to forgive would corrupt our humanity and twist our souls. She also said she was a little disappointed with the low numbers of people registering for counselling.

'If this is pride,' she said, 'pride comes before a fall. Don't be afraid to talk.' Then she made an offer that I at least couldn't refuse. 'Tomorrow, after lunch, Mrs Joseph has agreed to give up some of her time to come and speak to you. This will not be an assembly address, this will not be a lecture or a lesson, this will be an informal session for you to speak to her, ask her any questions, within reason, and get to know her. This was her idea – Mrs Joseph has made it clear that she wishes to keep strong ties to the school, and I think it could be an alternative to counselling for many of you. So that's tomorrow after lunch. Those of you that want to go should let your head of year know today.'

At lunchtime I went to register for the session with Mrs Joseph, and as I was leaving the classroom where the registration was taking place I met Warren Stanmore. Warren was a quiet kid and famous at school for being good at everything. There were rumours that he was only clever because he had private lessons after school, but he insisted that he didn't, he said that he just paid attention in class and got his work done.

'What are you doing in there?' he asked me.

'I'm going to that thing with Mrs Joseph. Why don't you come?'

'What's the point?'

Good question I thought. 'I'm not sure,' I said. 'I just want to know more about her, man. She's been through a lot, you know.'

'I know. But she said she don't want anyone feeling sorry for her. You heard her.'

'Yeah,' I said. 'I heard her, but she wants to get to know us better, and we should know her better. Who knows, she may just talk about football tomorrow, or swimming. Someone told me she's into swimming.'

Warren wasn't convinced. 'I can't be doing all that workshop stuff. I think it's sad what happened to Mr Joseph but I could see it coming.'

Then I remembered. For a short time Warren was quite close to Lionel and Ramzi. No one could understand why they had become friends, he was so different from them, but friends they were, and although the friendship didn't last for long it surprised us all.

'Yeah, that's right,' I said. 'I remember now. You used to hang out with them.'

Warren got defensive. 'I didn't really hang out with them, they were trying to hang out with me. I would just mind my own business and they would come and ask me to do things with them.'

'So what kind of things did you do?' I asked.

'Weird things.'

'Weird things like what?'

Warren lowered his gaze as he began to recall.

'One day the three of us took it in turns to stare at each other to see who could outstare who.'

'I've done that,' I said. 'That's not weird. People do that all the time.'

'No, but if you were the first to look away you'd have to bite the fingernails of the others.'

'That is a bit weird,' I conceded.

'And then one day,' he continued, 'one day we all

had to write down which teachers we hated most, and then we had to suggest ways of torturing them.'

'Now that's weird,' I said. 'Who did you suggest?'

Warren got very defensive again. 'I can't remember. I wasn't taking it all that seriously, you know. I don't think they were that serious either, they were just weird people, man, couldn't you see that?'

'Yeah. I knew they were weird, but I just didn't know how weird.'

'Do you remember the way they would just stare at people? I saw Lionel do that to a copper once. The copper just stopped and searched us, said we looked suspicious. Ramzi even got stop-searched on the day of the killing.'

Now that surprised me.

'How do you know?' I asked.

'Because I passed by when it was happening. They didn't find anything on him, so nothing happened, but then I saw him ten minutes later staring at a dog.'

'A dog?' I yelled.

'Yeah, a dog, almost nose to nose. That's what I'm saying, he was weird, both of them were weird.'

Warren raised his eyes but then he looked past me down the corridor and then over his back as if he was going to pass on classified information to me.

'If you want to see how weird meet me after school and I'll show you something, I'll show you weird.'

'I'll meet you.'

'OK. Straight after last lesson, outside the main gate.'

I got on with the rest of the day and met Warren at the main gate and he began to walk. I just followed him.

'So where are we going?' I asked.

'Just follow me.'

'What's this weird thing, then?'

'You'll see.'

Somehow we began talking about food. We were comparing the kind of food our parents cooked for us to the kind of food we liked and bought ourselves, when I realised that we were just two streets away from Fentham Road, the road where Lionel used to live, Carla and Jason's road, the road with the gang that didn't like me round their ends.

'Stop,' I said. 'You ain't taking me down that Fentham Road, are you? They're some kids down there that just go for me every time they see me. And they've only seen me twice.'

'No,' he said. 'Don't worry. I know who you're talking about. No, we're going down here.'

We turned down the street that ran parallel with Fentham Road and when we got about halfway down we stopped and he knocked on a door. A woman in her late sixties opened the door; she looked very pleased to see Warren.

'Hello, Warren, my love,' she said happily. 'It's so wonderful to see you, do come in. Who's your friend?'

'This is Jackson,' Warren said as we entered the house.

'Hello, Jackson. Well, my name's Norma, and this is my little house. I was born here. Not many people can say that about their house when they're my age.'

That impressed me. 'What, you were actually born here?'

'That's right,' she said proudly. 'In the room above where we are standing now, over half a century ago. Would you like some tea or a cold drink?'

'No thanks, I'm OK,' I replied.

'I'm OK too, Norma,' said Warren. 'How's your pain?'

'Not too bad, as long as I keep moving. Arthritis doesn't like the cold, the damp, or a lazy body.'

Warren began to look around. 'Where's Trinidad, Norma?'

Why is he asking her where a Caribbean island is? I wondered.

'He's outside,' she replied. 'He's OK. Do you want to see him?'

'If that's all right,' said Warren.

We went into the back garden, where a beautiful silver cat was lying down at the far end.

Norma began making kissing noises and hissing

gently. The cat stood up and began to walk towards me.

'This is Trinidad. What do you notice about him?' asked Warren.

I watched the cat carefully. It staggered towards us, struggling to keep its balance.

'It's drunk,' I said.

'Look carefully,' said Warren.

'I'm looking. It's drunk, or maybe it hasn't woke up yet.'

Warren began to sound like a teacher. 'Look even more carefully. Can't you see?'

'Can't I see what?'

Warren gave in. 'Look at his tail.'

I looked, and it didn't have one. 'Where's his tail?' I said loudly.

'Lionel Ferrier cut it off,' said Warren.

'He what?' I shouted.

'He cut it off, man. Just for a laugh, just for a stupid laugh. That's more than weird, that's sick. This wasn't the first cat either.' He pointed over the back fence. 'You see that house there, that's Lionel's house, that's where he lives. One day we were in his back yard, all these cats were passing through, he gave us an axe and he dared me and Ramzi to get a cat and cut off its tail. Ramzi caught a cat and went to cut its tail off but he didn't do it properly, he got a bit of its tail and he cut into one of its back legs. That cat screamed with pain and Lionel just laughed. Then he told me to have a go. I took the axe but I couldn't do it. He went mad. He took the axe from me and started waving it at me. Just then Trinidad was passing and Lionel started going on about how he hated this cat, and that cats and women are bad, and how they both get on his nerves. So he started calling Trinidad and Trinidad just came to him, thinking he was going to stroke him or something. That Lionel's got no feelings, he just got hold of Trinidad by the back of the neck, put his foot on his tail and cut it off.'

It was as if Trinidad knew we were talking about him. He came up to me and started rubbing himself on my leg. The story horrified me.

'Oh, man, that's evil,' I said, looking down at the cat. Now I couldn't miss the fact that he had no tail.

'He's evil,' said Warren.

'I'm just glad Trinidad's alive,' said Norma, coming up behind us. 'Look at him. After what he's been through you would have thought he would hate humans, but he's such a loving cat, such a forgiving cat.'

CHAPTER 9

A Meeting of Minds

As Warren and I walked home he told me how he got to know where Trinidad lived and how he went round to confess and apologise to Norma. Since then they had become good friends. She had been moved by his willingness to face up to what he had been a part of and he had been moved by her willingness to forgive. He told me of other strange things that Lionel and Ramzi had done, things like throwing car battery acid at animals, making small explosives and setting them off on wastelands, and pretending to shoot passers-by with toy guns. I was beginning to feel like I was getting somewhere. It was not much, but I was beginning to know more about Lionel and Ramzi. This was just the start of my therapy.

There was a very low turn-out at Mrs Joseph's session. There were about twenty of us to start with but after about ten minutes five people walked out. But I was so interested in what she had to say that I had to stay and listen. She spent much of the time talking about her hobbies, and about her days in school. She had obviously made a decision not to dwell on the killing. Although she wasn't very funny it was also very obvious that she was trying to make us laugh. I had come to the conclusion that this was her way of dealing with the empty space that was now in her life. As I stood trying to laugh at her jokes I looked around and thought that maybe what she was trying to do was create a new family for herself.

After the session I managed to speak with Mrs Joseph. This time it was much easier, Mrs Martel wasn't watching over her. I thanked her for coming to talk to us.

'Did you enjoy it?' she asked.

'Yeah. It was great, really interesting, and much better than history. Well, it was a kind of history lesson wasn't it?' I said, trying to sound intelligent.

'History, yes, but a lesson, no.'

Trying to sound super-intelligent I put on my thinking face and muttered, 'We're always making history, and lessons must be learnt from history. History is always about to happen.'

Mrs Joseph smiled. 'Did you read that somewhere?'

'No, I just made it up, and it probably doesn't really make sense, but that doesn't make it a lie. My intentions are good.'

'Very impressive.'

I wasn't sure if she was really impressed or just trying not to make me look stupid.

'All I'm trying to say is it was a good session. You were saying some cool things.'

'Thank you,' she said. 'It's nice to know that I'm being appreciated.'

Now this was like one of those moments that happens in movies, we had to take the conversation somewhere else. If I were older I would be asking her out for dinner, but I wasn't, so trying to be professional I asked, 'You really are not bitter at all, are you, miss?'

She tilted her head as if I had asked her out for dinner and said, 'First of all, you don't have to call me miss. It's Mrs Joseph, or Mary. And second, I'm not bitter because I know that it's not as simple as it seems, there's a back story to all this. Those boys just didn't turn up from nowhere as evil kids out to kill my husband. There's more to it. I don't know what it is, but I'm beginning to find out.'

On hearing this I was convinced that we were thinking along the same lines, so I thought it was a good moment to suggest something that I had been thinking about for some time.

'Miss,' I said. 'Sorry, I mean, Mrs Joseph. Could I have a word with you privately?'

She pointed in the direction of the classroom. 'Let's go back in there.'

We sat on the desks facing each other. She looked around as if to make a final check that we were alone, and then she asked in a low voice. 'OK. What's the problem?'

'You just said that those boys just didn't turn up from nowhere as evil kids and that you were beginning to find out more about them. Well, I feel the same. I know they were a bit weird but I want to know how they got weird, and I want to know more. I have started my own little investigation and I think we should join forces. You know, share information.'

Her face became very stiff and there was a tremor in her voice as she replied.

'This is not a game, young man. It is nice to know that you care but this is not like a game of hide-and-seek.'

'I know, Mrs Joseph. I'm not treating it like a game, really, I'm not.'

She clenched her fist and her face grew hard.

'The police have got involved because that's their job. I'm involved because one half of my life has been taken away. Why do you want to get involved? What do you have to gain?'

I was now very nervous. I knew that if I said the wrong thing I would lose her trust for ever. It was the turn for my voice to tremble.

'It's not really about me gaining anything, although it could help. I know he was your husband but I was really shocked by what I saw. I just can't stop thinking about it, it keeps replaying in my mind. I don't want that counselling they offered but I just know that understanding it all will help me, and like you I think there's more to it. Most people think it's an open and shut case, Mr Joseph good guy, Ramzi Sanchin and Lionel Ferrier bad guys, bad guys get caught, go to jail, end of story, but I don't think it's as simple as that, and you don't think it's as simple as that either. I reckon me and you are the only people thinking like this, so let's put our heads together.'

'You're right, I don't think it's as simple, but why should I trust you?'

'I can't answer that. I can only say that I think you can find out things that can help me, and I'm sure that I can find out things that can help you. We have the same goal, we are seeking the same truth.'

'You take this very seriously,' she said very seriously.

'Yes I do.'

'This is my life and my death,' she said, looking straight into my mind. 'If you think the truth will help you, imagine what it would do for me. I'm going to trust you, young man, but the moment you start taking me, or my husband, for granted, the moment you start playing up, you lose me, you lose me as a partner, and you lose me as a friend. Do you understand me?

'Yes,' I said, nodding my head vigorously. 'I won't

let you down.'

The buzzer sounded. It was time for the next lesson and I could hear pupils coming our way.

'Miss,' I said hurriedly. 'Mrs Joseph. Thanks.'

'Have you got a pen?' she asked.

I gave her a pen from my jacket pocket and she quickly wrote something on a scrap of paper.

'There you go. That's my home phone number, my mobile number and my email address. Get in touch one way or another. If we are going to work together we should start soon. I'd be really interested to hear what you've found out.'

I took it from her and stood up. 'Thanks. I have to go. I'll be in touch soon. I've got a mobile, would you like my number?'

'Yes.'

'It's 07945 –' She was just looking at me so I stopped. 'What's the matter? Don't you want to write it down?'

'No,' she replied. 'Just tell me and I'll remember it'.

'You will?'

'I will,' she said, so I told her, and she continued to look at me as she logged it in her brain.

As I was leaving a group of girls were entering the classroom to start their lesson. They gave us strange looks as if we were up to something dodgy, but my conscience was clear. I was just doing my job.

CHAPTER 10

Rendezvous by the Pool

Although my mother followed the story of Mr Joseph's murder, what she really wanted was the tabloid version. This wasn't tabloid, though, this one was happening in her neighbourhood, and her son had witnessed it. The case was beginning to take over my life. I had always had an enquiring mind. When I was younger I went through a stage when all questions were about clouds, then I moved on to lightning, then snow, then trains. As I grew up I began to ask questions about cities, who planned them, who policed them, and who policed the police that policed them? All this made it easy for my mother to think that 'my investigation' was just another of my passing interests, a small chapter in my intellectual development. But I needed to tell her this was more that that. I told her what I had heard about Lionel and Ramzi, and I filled her in on my conversations with Mrs Joseph.

'I'm on a mission, Mum.'

'We're all on a mission, son. My mission is to get a winning lottery ticket, I've just got to walk into the right newsagent at the right time and everything will fall into place. What's your mission?'

'I want to find the truth.'

'Well,' she replied, as if talking to a naughty boy, 'if you do well in school and you go on to university you could study philosophy, and then you could find the truth.'

'No, Mum,' I huffed in frustration. 'I want to find out the truth about Mr Joseph's killing. I call it "the case".'

'Yes, Jackson, it's a police case, and that's it.'

'It's my case too. I was there when it happened; there were no police there then. I saw it with my own eyes, but I know there's more to this than meets the eye.'

My mother gestured towards the television that was turned on with the sound muted.

'I think you've been watching too many detective films.'

'This is serious, Mum. I may be employing the techniques of a detective but I have to get to the bottom of this. I need to do it for myself and in the name of justice.'

Her laugh told me that she wasn't sure if she should be taking me seriously or not.

'Employing the techniques of a detective? In the name of justice? Why don't you chase a football or chase girls like other boys? I'm the only mother I know who has a son that goes into his room to think. If you're an Einstein or a Sherlock Holmes let me know. Come out of the closet now, I'll stick by you.'

'No, Mum, I don't have any genius to declare, I just have a bit of detective work to do.'

'OK. You do your detective work but you be careful. This is murder, not a missing mobile phone. Don't go upsetting people, and don't start making enemies.'

Knowing that my mother was OK with what I was doing, if not over the moon was good, and knowing that Mrs Joseph was on my side was also a great boost, so I wasted no time getting in touch with her. The day after she gave me her numbers I called her and we arranged to meet after school in the café of the local sports centre. I turned up right on time; she was already there reading a newspaper and eating a sandwich. She looked bright, a little wet, but bright.

'How long have you been here?' I asked.

'A couple of hours,' she replied. 'I've been swim-ming. I go when I can, and just lately I've been going a lot. Swimming is a kind of meditation. I find that when I swim I forget about everything else. I have to; if I start thinking about anything else my technique goes to pot. Can I get you a drink?

I saw that she was drinking something that was bright orange.

'I'll have some of that, whatever it is.'

She stood up, and just before she turned to go to the drinks counter she handed me the newspaper.

'Have a read.'

Somehow the newspaper had found out about the classroom talk that Mrs Joseph had given the day before. The article was full of exaggerations, it talked about a classroom packed full of eager pupils. I wasn't sure how eagerness was measured, because they failed to mention the pupils that walked out. It said she talked passionately about how she was coping with losing her husband, but I was there all the time and as far as I recall she didn't mention him once. It described her as glamorous, well, that's cool, that's how I describe my mum, but, it also described her as a wise widow, now that was strange. The term 'a wise widow' made me think of witches, and fortune-tellers, and spiders.

Mrs Joseph came back, handed me the bright orange drink and said, 'Great, isn't it? Last week I was a wilting housewife in mourning, this week I'm a glamorous wise widow. Maybe I should call them and ask them who I'm going to be next week.' She was smiling, I wasn't.

'How do they get stories like this, how can they get away with printing that stuff?' I moaned.

'It has to be what they called "leaked", by a so-called mole. In other words a spy.'

Now I was smiling.

'Come off it. You really think that there was a spy in there yesterday?'

'A spy is maybe too sophisticated a word, but there was definitely someone in there who went and talked to the press.'

I sipped the bright orange drink. It burnt my stomach.

'Do you think they got paid for it?'

'No, I doubt it,' she replied. 'I'm not that important. Can you swim?'

We talked for while about keeping fit, keeping sane, and keeping pets, then I got on to my subject.

'Thanks for seeing me. Where shall we start?'

'I'll start,' she said. 'I don't know much about Lionel, but Ramzi Sanchin doesn't live that far from me and I've been doing my own little investigation. Ramzi doesn't have a birth certificate.'

I was confused. 'So, what's that mean? what's that got to do with anything?'

'He was found in a telephone box. He doesn't know who his parents are, he doesn't know where he was born, he doesn't know if his parents ever gave him a name, and he doesn't even know his real birthday. He was front-page news when he was found and people from all over the country were offering to give him a home. In the end he was given one by a wealthy well-connected family. As he started to grow up and his new family realised that he wasn't going to be the dream baby they had in mind they washed their hands of him. Basically they gave him back to the social services. He was then put into a care home for a couple of years and then fostered out. He has gone from foster home to foster home; from what I've worked out he's never stayed in one home for more than two years. He was named after the first doctor to examine him after he was found.'

'Not a good start,' I said.

'Not at all. He hasn't been abused as far as I know, but I hear he's always acted like there was a part of him missing, he's always been a bit withdrawn. Most of the foster parents meant well, but he didn't really connect with them. Lionel was the first friend he had.'

'Interesting,' I replied. 'I've been checking out Lionel Ferrier.'

'Did you know him before?'

'I knew him,' I said cautiously, 'but I didn't know much about him, except that if you lent him something he would probably break it and not care. What I know now is that he's a bit dark. He used to make his friends play strange games with him and if you lost to someone you'd have to bite their nails. He liked torture treatments; he used to try to imagine the worse torture treatments he could. He used to pretend to shoot people with toy guns, anybody, you know, just people passing by, and you won't believe this, he used to cut cats' tails off.'

Up until then Mrs Joseph was looking interested, now she was looking shocked.

'He cut cats' tails off? What for? What did he do with them?'

'Nothing as far as I know, he just did it for a laugh. I know where he lives, it's crazy around there. The kids patrol the street as if they own it, and everyone knows everyone's business. But Lionel didn't really get on with the other kids at school, he was a loner, and his mum had a bit of a reputation.'

'A reputation for what?'

'I'm not sure, really. I'm just told she had a reputation. She was a bit of a loner too.'

'There are all kinds of reputations. Maybe she's a wise widow and her wisdom is highly sought,' said Mrs Joseph sarcastically.

'I don't know,' I replied. 'I'm only going by what people tell me.'

Mrs Joseph leaned forwards and put her elbows on the table.

'You have done quite a bit of work, haven't you?

'I have my sources.'

'And you're so enthusiastic.'

'I'm fired up at the moment because I hate the way it's being reported in the newspapers.'

'Yes, the evil press. But if you really want to know more you have to also realise that even the stuff that people tell you can be wrong. People have their prejudices. Especially when it comes to women. Just because a woman has no friends it doesn't mean that

55

her son is a born killer. Look at this.' She pointed to the newspaper. 'Just because I sat in front of a group of kids it doesn't make me a wise woman.'

'I know,' I said. 'That's why I'm trying to separate the facts from the hearsay, that's why I'm going to step up my investigations. I'm going to go round and talk to Lionel's mum. I'm going to tell her I'm on her side and speak to her face to face.'

Mrs Joseph sat back on the chair. 'Are you sure?'

'Why not? Do you mind?

'No, it's your move, but it has its risks.'

'Yes I know, but why not get it straight from the horse's mouth? It makes sense to me. Hey, why don't you come?'

'No, I couldn't, and what would I say to her? "I'd like to know more about your son, it would help me and my friend Jackson." I don't think so. Anyway, don't forget there's a court case and I can't be seen to be interfering with what a judge may see as the other side. But you, you're a free agent.'

We spent an hour together in all and I came away refreshed and full of energy. Mrs Joseph stayed on at the sports centre to go to a Bums, Tums and Thighs class, whatever that was. As I was leaving we shook hands, which made me feel as if I had sealed some kind of deal, or was going on a dangerous mission.

'Be careful,' she said. 'And don't start investigating me, not without my permission, anyway.'

CHAPTER 11

It Looks Like Rain

I wasn't sure how to go about doing it but I was determined to go and see Lionel's mother that evening. I didn't have a phone number, so I thought the only thing I could do was walk up to the door and knock on it, but I didn't even know the number of her house. I could have walked down Fentham Road and tried to judge where Norma's house was and from there work out where Lionel's house was, but that was leaving too much to chance, especially in hostile territory. I decided to go back and see Norma. She greeted me as if we were old friends, and so did Trinidad. Apparently when he really likes you he leaves large amounts of his fur on your trouser legs. He did that to me. Norma gave me a handful of sweets and Lionel's house number. I stroked Trinidad, took a handful of his fur, and left.

My immediate concern was the possibility of walking into that gang. As I walked around the block I noticed that I was chewing my lips, and as I got closer to the road I chewed more hungrily. When I reached Fentham Road I was ready to eat myself, but I was surprised to find the road relatively quiet. A bit of music could be heard, the dogs were barking quietly, and overall the street was quite welcoming. Walking down it I was half expecting the gang to jump out at me, but no, it was all so easy.

Thirty-five Fentham Road looked like any other house on the street. I rang the bell; it was so loud it made me jump. I heard someone coming. The person stopped behind the door, listening or peeping, I thought. A woman's voice came from behind the door.

'Who is it?'

'Hello. My name's Jackson, Jackson Jones. Could I have a word with you?

'You're a bit young for a salesman. What are you trying to sell me?'

I couldn't see her but somehow she could see me. 'I'm not trying to sell you anything, I'm not a salesman, I'm a pupil from Marston Hall school.'

'Oh no, not another one. Listen, I'm not in the mood for any of your pranks. I've had enough of you kids.'

I thought that distancing myself from whoever had been bothering her would help.

'I promise you, Mrs Ferrier, I am not another one of those kids. I've never done any silly pranks, I have more important things to do. I'm just fed up of all the crazy rumours that I'm hearing and I just wanted to talk with you.'

'Why? Are you a little detective, a baby cop? Is

your daddy a cop? What do you want to talk about?'

I didn't want to be too specific. 'I used to be a friend of Lionel's. Do you remember he came home with an MP3 music player thing? I lent him that, we were mates. I just wanted to talk to you about a few things.'

'Go away,' she said.

'Honestly, Mrs Ferrier, I won't be long.'

'It's Miss Ferrier, and I said go away.'

'Please,' I pleaded.

'I said go away now before the weather changes.'

A strange thing to say, I thought. 'I'm not worried about the weather,' I said. 'I promise you I won't be –'

'Go,' she interrupted. 'Go now or else.'

'OK,' I said. 'I'm going. But please remember my name, Jackson Jones. Really, I'm not one of those kids that play pranks.'

'Go,' she said again firmly.

I walked for a few metres then stopped. I thought about what she had said. She had obviously been troubled by kids in the past and so she was understandably wary of all kids. I was convinced that if I could win her trust we could be useful to each other. She could help me understand her son, and I could help her out of her isolation. I decided to go back and try again. If she wasn't going to speak to me I was going to leave a note for her with ways of contacting me. I thought maybe she would change her mind if she had a bit of time.

I rang the bell again. I heard her approach.

'Who is it?' she asked.

'It's me, Jackson, again.'

'You again.'

In an attempt to get a dialogue going I said, 'I have an idea, Miss Ferrier.'

She quickly interrupted me.

'I have an idea too,' she said. 'Wait a moment.'

I could hear her moving around as if looking for a key.

'Just hold on one minute,' she said.

Pleased by her change of heart and my progress I stood smiling to myself. I felt that this was a major breakthrough. She was taking her time but that was cool, this was worth the wait. Then I heard a voice from above me.

'Hello.'

I looked up and saw a cloud with a golden lining, and then I was slapped in the face with two litres of urine. Piss, medium-warm piss, all over me.

'There you are,' she said. 'The weather's changed.'

As I realised what she meant there was laughter behind me. Across the road was the gang I feared so much, laughing and congratulating me on my warm-shower award.

I didn't know if I should run or walk. I walked, and that gang of kids walked behind me all the way down the road, reminding me of how the weather had taken a change for the worse, and assuring me that I was not the first to get caught without an umbrella.

CHAPTER 12

The Weather Report

It took me a long time to recover from that storm. For days afterwards I could smell the insides of Miss Ferrier everywhere I went. My mother could smell it too. I didn't tell her about it but I could see that she had checked my sheets to see if I had been wetting my bed, and I knew for sure she suspected something when just before saying goodnight to me she asked, 'How's your health, son?'

'Just fine', I replied. 'No changes.'

'No boy problems?'

'No, Mum, no boy problems,' I said defensively.

'Well, son, you know you can speak to me if you have any problems. I mean that, you know. Any problems at all, you can speak to me.'

'Yes, Mum, goodnight, Mum.'

But it was pretty bad. I could smell that stuff as I slept, I could smell it as I washed, every time I took a drink I was reminded of that wet evening. I had urine on my mind and to make things worse I felt that my schoolwork was beginning to suffer. I wasn't doing too bad, but I knew I wasn't concentrating as much as I should have been and I felt that if I wasn't going to draw attention to myself from my teachers and my mother, I had to make sure that my schoolwork wasn't affected. I took a few days off from my investigations to get back to normality and recover from my humiliation. I washed a lot, and studied hard, but although I wasn't actively making enquires I couldn't stop my mind from asking questions.

I gave it a week, and then I put myself back on the case. First I wanted to see Mrs Joseph. I called her and we decided to meet at the same place, at the same time. I declined the offer to go swimming.

When I got to the sports centre there she was, reading a newspaper and eating.

'Hello, Jackson. Good to see you. Sit down. Can I get you a drink?'

I thought about it. I didn't fancy that bright orange stuff I had before, and when I looked towards the drinks counter the gold-coloured drinks on display reminded too much of my last encounter with liquid of that colour.

'No,' I said. 'I'm fine.'

I sat down, and she put the newspaper down and did that elbows-on-the-table, leaning-forward thing.

'Guess what,' she said, taking a glance around like a secret agent in a movie. 'I found out some really interesting stuff. I didn't go looking for it, it came to me via a neighbour.'

'Yeah. What?'

'Last year this woman turned up out of the blue asking loads of questions and really upsetting Ramzi and his foster parents.'

'How?'

'Well, at first she just turned up at the house, and hung around outside his school, generally making a nuisance of herself.'

'Why, what was she up to?' I asked.

'She was claiming to be Ramzi's mother. Ramzi didn't want to know. After a big row outside his house she was arrested and kept in a cell to cool off for a couple of hours.'

This was really interesting for my investigation. Mrs Joseph was visibly excited.

'When they let her out of the station did she just disappear?' I asked.

'No,' said Mrs Joseph. 'She came back the next day demanding that Ramzi go and live with her. Ramzi wasn't having it, he said that there's no way that she could be his mother and he wasn't going anywhere with her. She went away and came back another day a little bit drunk, but this time Ramzi's foster mother called the police and social services. A policewoman and a social worker turned up and told her to leave them alone. They threatened to put an injunction on her.'

'What's an injunction?' I asked. It was important that I understood every word of this.

'It's basically a ban on someone; usually they say you can't go within a certain amount of miles radius of this or that place or person. So they warned her and then told her that if she really wanted to take it further she should speak to the social services. The social worker even gave her a card with telephone numbers on it.'

'And?' I couldn't wait to hear how it ended.

'And nothing, she was never seen again.'

An anti-climax, I thought. 'She just said forget it?'

'Well, no one knows if she was serious or just a bit mad. The point is she never came back. Are you sure you don't want a drink?'

Her story may have had no real ending, but what did I have to report? Very little. As I declined the drink I was trying to think of a way into the very little that I had to say. Mrs Joseph prompted me. 'What have you been up to?'

'Nothing much,' I replied, still thinking.

'I can't imagine you doing nothing much.'

'I've been trying to catch up on my schoolwork.'

'Oh yes,' she said. 'Can't forget your schoolwork.'

'After we spoke the last time I did go round to see Lionel's mum.'

She sounded surprised. 'You did?'

'Yeah, I did.'

'Well, tell me what happened. What did she say?'

I nervously began folding and unfolding the corners of her newspaper.

'She told me to go away, and she threw some water over me.'

She sounded even more surprised. 'She threw water over you? Oh my God. What kind of water?

'Water,' I said. 'You know, water.'

'Yes, but what kind of water?'

'Used water,' I said. 'Used water.' I really didn't know what to say to her, this was the best I could do without lying.

'You mean she was washing the dishes and she threw the dishwater over you?'

'No,' I said. 'She drank the water, it passed through her, and then she threw it over me. It was urine. Piss.'

'I know,' she said, smiling.

Now I was surprised. 'Hey, you knew all the time. How did you know?

'People are talking. What happened is some kid from Fentham Road told some kid on my street and that kid told me. They didn't know your name, they just said someone had this encounter with this woman on this night, and I knew it was you. Apparently she's famous for doing it, she does a kind of weather warning, or weather forecast, and if she doesn't get things her way she gives you a soaking. Apparently the police came round once to talk to her about it and she gave them a soaking too.'

That hour with Mrs Joseph wasn't so pleasant. Telling her about my warm shower was embarrassing enough, but it was more embarrassing finding out that she already knew. Once again she stayed on to do her Bums, Tums and Thighs class and I went home, to cry – internally of course, I don't do crying aloud.

CHAPTER 13

Stranger Danger

When I went home that afternoon my mum handed me a letter. It was addressed to her, but it was about me. The letter informed her that the case against Lionel and Ramzi was to be heard in court during the summer holiday in just over a week and I was being called as a witness. I was given two options, I could stand up in court and give evidence, or because of my age and what they called the sensitive nature of the case, I could simply submit the written statement that I had already made to the police. I wasn't sure what to do. I stood there thinking aloud, saying, 'Should I go, or shouldn't I?'

My mother said that she didn't doubt my ability to stand up in court and say my piece, but she also thought that if the statement I had already given was sufficient and I had nothing to add then it wasn't necessary for me to stand in front of people and repeat it. Still, in her wisdom, she left it up to me, telling me she trusted my judgement. I thought about it for a couple of hours and when it began to give me a headache I rang Mrs Joseph. She had also arrived home to find a letter notifying her of the date of the hearing, but in effect she was just a spectator. I told her that I wanted to see as much of the trial as possible and then she made an interesting suggestion. The defendants and most of the witnesses were going to be juveniles, which meant it would be a closed court. She reckoned that if I appeared as a witness I would only be able to enter the courtroom at the time I gave my evidence, but if I submitted a written statement I could be her companion and that would allow me to sit in the courtroom throughout the trial. A brilliant idea, I thought. I would have thought of it myself if I had given myself a bit more time, but there was a problem. My mother didn't like the idea.

'Going to court to give evidence is one thing,' she said, 'but going everyday with a strange woman is another. I'm not saying she's bad or anything, but you hardly know her. And what will she think of me letting my son out with a stranger?'

'Mum, we're going to court, not on a date,' I said, sounding as if I'd been on many a date. 'What's wrong with that?'

'It doesn't look good.'

'It's not about looks, Mum, it's about justice,' I said, sounding like an expert on justice.

She looked towards the ceiling for a while as if

looking for an idea, then she found one.

'OK. You can go if you let me speak to her first.'

'Mum,' I shouted. 'I'm not a child.'

'You are,' she replied. 'You're my child.'

I couldn't argue with that. I went and wrote down Mrs Joseph's phone number for her and then I went for a walk. For some reason I didn't want to be in the house while they were talking about me on the phone. When I came back my mother started playing mind games with me.

'I need to tell you something,' she said, pointing to a seat.

I sat down.

'You are still my child.'

'I know that,' I said.

'So what I have to say is final.'

'Yes, Mum.'

'You can go,' she said, smiling. 'I had a talk with Mrs Joseph and she seems like a really nice woman. I was very impressed with her. Dignified, that's what I'd call her, dignified.

The next day I had another talk with Warren Stanmore. He was becoming very useful. He told me about other strange deeds committed by Lionel and Ramzi. Some of them were just the usual pranks like putting glue into door locks, and scaring people at night in the local graveyard, whilst others were more bizarre, like risking their lives walking on the ledges of high buildings, or catching birds and keeping them prisoner for days as they watched them starve to death. He had story after story, and I had no reason to doubt the authenticity of them. He had no axe to grind. He also knew about my meeting with Lionel's mum, and he told me that Norma knew. From then on I assumed that everyone knew.

'Thanks,' I said, and I began to walk away.

'Hey, are you going, then?' he asked.

'Going where?'

'Going to court,' he said.

'So you know about that too? I'm going all right, it was a bit iffy but I'm going. It's difficult to explain now but –'

I was in full flow when I felt an almighty slap across the back of my head. I turned and there were these two boys with who I presumed were their girlfriends hanging on their arms. I recognised one of them; it was Terry Stock, the new school bully. All of them stood there grinning at me.

'What's your problem? What did you do that for?' I said, high-pitched and surprised.

Terry started. 'You think you're a private investigator or something, hey. What's your game? Who do you think you are, poking your nose around?'

'I know who I am. What's your game? What you do that for? I replied.

'You should mind your own business,' said the other boy.

'Yeah,' said one girl.

'Yeah, that's right,' said the other.

'I was minding my own business,' I said. 'We were just talking and you came here and hit me, one of you did. We were just –' I looked back to Warren but he wasn't there.

'We who?' said one the girls.

I gave in. 'Ah, forget it. I don't get you lot.'

'But we got you,' said Terry. 'And we'll get you again.'

I left them standing there and that was that. I didn't know if this was Terry and his gang just being boys showing off or if it was the start of a reign of terror, they'd demanded no goods or favours from me. All I knew was that I wasn't going to stand for it. And where was Warren when I needed him? He was a good informant, but he was a bit of a chicken.

CHAPTER 14

We All Got Court

There were more stories in the newspapers and more stories in the playground, but then the summer holidays began and not much happened until the court case started. The night before the first day of the trial was so hot that I hardly slept. I wanted to journey back to the winter. I saw the morning weather forecast on TV and it was all about the heat, but then there was my mum who insisted that I wear a suit to court. I didn't want to, but I did. I needed to keep her sweet. I only had one suit, and I'd only ever worn that once, to my grandfather's funeral. It was getting smaller and I was getting bigger, but I managed to squeeze into it. I felt I had to. My mother was so adamant that I wore a suit that she said if it didn't fit me she would go and buy me a new one. I didn't want her to waste her money, and more importantly, I didn't want to own another suit.

Mrs Joseph passed by to pick me up in a taxi as we had arranged and we headed for the court. When we arrived the taxi was immediately surrounded by press reporters. I'd expected some press but not that many, and I could see that Mrs Joseph was surprised too. After she paid the fare we sat in the taxi, not sure what to do. The taxi driver was reminding us that he had a job to do and that he didn't have time to sit around all day looking at us when the taxi door was opened by two men. One of them opened his arms to create some space for us.

'Good morning,' he said cheerfully. 'We're court staff.'

Like a well-rehearsed double act the other one said, 'We've been asked to help you in. Don't worry about that lot. Just say nothing, and come with us.'

We did as we were told. As we walked from the taxi to the court they shielded us from the reporters who shouted questions at Mrs Joseph. I wasn't sure how they expected her to answer questions like, 'How are you coping after the death of your husband?' or, 'What kind of verdict are you looking for, Mrs Joseph?'

We put our heads down and walked in. I don't know about Mrs Joseph but the flashing lights made me feel more like a celebrity at a film premiere than a citizen heading for the public gallery of a murder trial.

We were taken to the courtroom. It was a modern extension to the old courthouse, and by the time we arrived there it was already quite full. We found two empty seats next to each other and sat down. There was a tap on my shoulder. I looked around, it was Mrs Martel.

'I knew you'd be here,' she said, smiling down on me like a guardian headmistress.

And I replied, 'I knew you'd be here,' believing that being outside of school allowed me to be a bit more imaginative with my responses to her.

'Now now,' she said. She turned to Mrs Joseph. 'Hello, Mary. I see he brought you along.'

Mrs Joseph replied politely and then the chatter that had filled the courtroom stopped. Someone shouted 'all stand', and we all stood. Three judges entered, one woman, with a man either side of her. They took a second to look ahead, then they sat. We took a second to watch them sit, then we sat. It was all a bit robotic. The clerk made an announcement informing us that this was a case of the state against two juveniles, and then the female judge spoke.

'Those of you in this room are here because you have some connection to the case. We have allowed in a limited number of members of the press, and I would firstly like to remind them that we are the judges here. You must make your reports, but you must report responsibly. Furthermore I want to remind all of you that the defendants in this case are juveniles, and so unless we grant permission to reveal their names you must protect their identities to the best of your abilities. It is important that everyone in this room understands this. Please bring the defendants in.'

There was absolute silence as Lionel and Ramzi were brought in by four uniformed police officers. They stood in front of seats behind small desks for a short while with an officer to the side and behind each of them. They were both dressed in their school uniforms, both looking pale and thin. They were ordered to sit. I looked to my right and saw a woman looking at me. She looked familiar, but I just couldn't place her. I looked away for a moment then I looked back. She was still looking at me. I looked a third time. Now she was looking straight ahead. There was something about her, but I couldn't work out what it was.

The female judge read out the charges.

'Lionel Ferrier, could you please stand. Lionel Ferrier, it is alleged that at three fifty-five, on April the twenty-fourth, of two thousand and seven, that you murdered Mr Edgar Arnold Joseph, in the grounds of Marston Hall school. How do you plead, guilty or not guilty?'

Lionel looked straight at the judge. 'Guilty.'

For thirty seconds no one spoke. All that could be heard was the woman who records every word typing away at her machine, the sound of pen upon paper as people took notes, and the sound of people breathing.

'Be seated,' said the judge. 'Ramzi Sanchin, could you please stand. Ramzi Sanchin, it is alleged that you conspired with Lionel Ferrier to commit an act of murder, that murder, of Mr Edgar Arnold Joseph, having been committed at three fifty-five, on April the twenty-fourth, of two thousand and seven, in the grounds of Marston Hall school. How do you plead, guilty or not guilty?'

Ramzi looked straight at the judge. 'Guilty.'

There was a repeat of the silent writing, and then Ramzi was told to sit down. The judges began to whisper amongst themselves when the silence was broken by a disturbance outside the courtroom. A woman was screaming and shouting at the top of her voice.

'Leave me alone! Why don't you believe me? I have a right to be in there, he's my son. He's my son. If my son's in court I have the right to be there. Now leave me alone.'

Lionel continued to stare straight ahead, but Ramzi looked disturbed. He began to look towards the direction of the shouting. Suddenly the door flew open and the two men who had brought me and Mrs Joseph in were chasing after a woman who was determined to sit in the court. She pointed to Ramzi.

'This is my son. You people don't know anything. He is innocent, and he is mine, and I have the right to be here.' She pointed to a man and a woman who were sitting behind Ramzi. 'You leave him alone – you keep your hands off my child. All this is your fault. He wouldn't be here if it wasn't for you, he wouldn't be here if you'd taken care of him. He's mine, my baby, mine.'

The couple remained motionless, we all remained motionless, all except for the two court staff who began trying to reason with her, but she just shouted above them.

One of the male judges spoke to the staff.

'Let me hear her speak.'

They stopped shouting at her, she stopped screaming, and the judge continued.

'You do realise that I could have you charged with contempt of court. What do you have to say for yourself?'

The woman pointed to Ramzi. 'That's my son, which means I have the right to be here.'

The judge turned to Ramzi. 'Is this your mother?'

Ramzi shook his head.

'Could you speak, please?'

'No,' Ramzi said, looking straight at the judge.

'Where are your parents?' asked the judge.

Ramzi lifted his shoulders. The judges whispered to each other.

'OK. Where are your foster parents, or your guardians?' asked the judge.

Ramzi pointed to the couple. 'They are my foster parents.'

'But where are your biological parents?' asked the judge.

'I don't know,' said Ramzi. 'I don't know who my parents are.'

The woman screamed, 'How can you say that? Forget all them fancy words you know, I'm your mother, I'm the only one that cares about you. What are they doing to you? These people don't care about you, I care about you.'

'Silence,' shouted the judge. He then looked towards the couple. 'Do you know this person?'

The man replied, 'We have seen her before. She appears sometimes and makes these outrageous claims, and then she disappears. We understand that she has some mental health issues.'

The woman then charged towards the couple but was held back by the two men.

'Mental health issues!' she shouted. 'I'll give you mental heath issues. You're all mental, the lot of you. Give me my son. Come on, son, we're going home.'

'OK,' said the judge. 'I want you to leave this courtroom now. If you have parental claims on this boy you must go through the proper channels. This may be the place but this is not the time.'

The woman began to cry. 'He's mine, you can't have him. He's mine, and you are all devils. You're the ones with the mental health issues. Yeah. This is no court, this is a joke.'

'Remove her from the court, please,' said the female judge.

The two men then took her arms and held her in some fancy jujitsu arm locks and led her out. She was still shouting, and we could hear her shouting all the way out of the building.

'Right,' said the female judge, 'let's get on with the business in hand. 'Can the legal representatives of the juveniles both stand?'

Two young men stood up. The judge continued.

'I take it that court procedure has been explained to your clients?'

They both said, 'Yes.'

'And you are both happy with their guilty pleas?'

One of them replied, 'We are not happy with them, and we have tried to talk to them as much as we could. We have given them as much advice as legally possible but they both insist on entering guilty pleas.'

The judge looked towards Lionel and Ramzi.

'Do you understand that you are entering a guilty plea which cannot be changed at a later date?'

They both said, 'Yes.'

'These are serious charges. Are you happy with your legal representation?'

They both said, 'Yes.'

'And you wish to stick with your plea?'

Once more they both said, 'Yes.'

'In that case,' said the judge. 'There will be no

need to call any witnesses. We will review the reports and return at nine a.m. tomorrow morning for sentencing. If there is no other business we shall adjourn until tomorrow.'

It was quick and it was strange. The woman claiming to be the mother of Ramzi certainly caused some courtroom drama, but I was more surprised by the way that Lionel and Ramzi seemed to have no life left in them. They remained emotionless throughout the hearing; they just didn't seem to care about what was going to happen to them.

After the judges left the courtroom and people were collecting their belongings and making their way out, I saw the woman who had caught my eye earlier. I nudged Mrs Joseph.

'Who's that?' I asked.

'I have no idea,' she replied.

I looked behind me. Mrs Martel was still there.

'Mrs Martel. Who's that lady over there?'

'Don't you know who that is?' she replied. 'That's Miss Ferrier, Lionel's mother.'

'Didn't you recognise her?' asked Mrs Joseph.

'I didn't get a good look at her face,' I said, a little embarrassed. But I had a plan. When we had left the courtroom but were still in the court building, I left Mrs Joseph for a moment and went to Miss Ferrier. I knew it was going to be tough but it was my one chance.

'Miss Ferrier,' I said. 'Do you remember me? Jackson Jones.'

'I remember you,' she said. 'Most kids just want to shout at me and throw things at me. You were the one that said you wanted to talk to me, but you couldn't fool me, I've seen enough tricks in my time. Talk to me.'

'But Miss Ferrier, it wasn't a trick, I really did want to talk to you. I'm not like the other kids.'

'All kids are alike. No manners, no discipline, no anything.'

I smiled in an attempt to humour her. 'I got manners, lots of them, and discipline, I got that too. I've even got anything, or I'll do anything, anything to get to the truth.'

She looked at me as if to pity me. 'Why do you want the truth? What would you do with it?'

'I don't really know until I know what the truth is, but when I know, I know that I'll want others to know so that people will think about truth and not believe lies. That's the truth, Miss Ferrier.'

She looked at me wondering about what I had just said. I looked at her wondering about what I had just said.

She yawned. 'Are you clever or just full of fancy talk?'

'I'm just a kid trying to make sense of all this.'

'You want to talk to me that badly, do you?'

'I do, Miss Ferrier.'

She glanced around. 'I can't see what's so important about talking to me. I'm just a nobody.'

'I think you're a somebody, Miss Ferrier.'

The pitch in her voice changed. Instead of speaking at me she spoke to me.

'I understand that the kids on the street give you a hard time.'

'You understand right.'

'Come and see me Sunday morning, about nine. The street's empty then, they're all asleep.'

'Oh, thanks, Miss Ferrier, thanks so much.'

'Just make sure you come early or the kids will give you hell. They give me hell all the time.'

I thought for a moment. 'Will you promise not to give me a warm shower?'

'I don't promise anything,' she said, and walked away.

CHAPTER 15

Mr Edgar Arnold Joseph

After we left the court Mrs Joseph took me to a small restaurant in the same park that Lionel and Ramzi had been arrested in. We sat outside in the sunshine, which was good for her, she was wearing a light summer dress, but I was still fully suited. After five minutes in the midday sun it dawned on me. I wasn't in court any more, my mother was not with me, and I probably looked stupid. I took the jacket off, it was the least I could do.

We talked about the morning's events, both of us still completely confused by the woman claiming to be Ramzi's mother. Although she had no proof of her claim, in her own way she sounded very convincing. On the other hand it was believed that Ramzi was probably abandoned on the other side of the country. How would she have managed to track him down? After so many foster parents how would she have kept up with his movements?

I was very surprised by the boys' guilty pleas. They did the crime of course, there were so many witnesses who saw it, but I was surprised that their solicitors didn't convince them to enter some other plea. Something like manslaughter, or guilty due to diminished responsibility, but like Mrs Joseph said, that would mean admitting they were mad. The speed of the proceedings suited Mrs Joseph fine. In keeping with her ideas of celebrating life, she didn't want to sit through lots of stories describing the death of her husband from different angles; she wanted to be filled with positive memories. We had a small lunch that took for ever to eat due to her telling me the life and times of Edgar Arnold Joseph. Now I know everything about him.

She told me that he was born in a small city in the north of England and was an only child. His body was covered with scars that he gained from living dangerously on bombsites as a small kid. At the age of eight he listed his hobbies as climbing up difficult trees, crashing home-made go-karts, jumping off speeding roundabouts and swinging on swings, rolling down hills in dustbins, and getting lost. His ambition was to climb Mount Everest, or the Post Office Tower. When he was eleven years old he began to take his schoolwork very seriously and his parents and his teachers began to see how intelligent he was. He had a great head for figures and was fascinated with science and the way that things work. His parents thought that he would do even better in a different environment. They weren't rich but they worked hard and sent him to a boarding school. He hated it. He said it wasn't so much about the school and the way they taught, or the other pupils, it was about home. He just loved coming home at the end of the day. Which apparently was the way he was as a teacher. He loved going to school, but he also loved going home, and at a boarding school he couldn't come home at the end of the day. After one term he was taken out of boarding school and admitted back into his comprehensive school.

He left school with lots of qualifications in all the right places and went to study philosophy at a university in the south of England. He didn't like it there either. Nothing wrong with the south of England, nothing wrong with the university, it was just too far away from home again. One cold day, just before he left university, he was on campus when he met Mrs Joseph, or Mary Dowling as she was then. She was trespassing. Twice a week she would casually walk on to the campus and use the university gym. Just like a student. But she was never a student. Her education had ended after sixth form college and she had become a successful classical concert organiser. She made a lot of money and now considers herself semi-retired. In other words she said, 'I'll do a job if my heart's in it, or if the money's great.'

They got married just after Mr Joseph left

university, but soon after, tragedy struck. Mr Joseph's mother was killed in a car crash. His father lived for another eight years but then he died after suffering a stroke. At the time of his father's death Mr Joseph was working for a large management group. He had a fancy title but basically his job was to spy on other workers in the company. After the death of his father he decided that he wanted to do something meaningful, and so he went into teaching. From everything that Mrs Joseph told me, I could tell that they really did love each other, and he really loved teaching.

CHAPTER 16

No Comments

The next morning we did exactly as we did the previous day. I was picked up in a taxi by Mrs Joseph, the press were waiting at the court, and the same two strong men walked us in. Inside the courtroom were most of the people who were there the day before, most of them sitting in the same seats. The seats we chose were almost the same, and Mrs Martel was in exactly the same place, right behind me. Miss Ferrier had moved position and was now sitting next to Ramzi's foster parents, right behind where the boys would be.

The judges came in, we stood up, they sat down, and we sat down. There was something about this ritual that I found amusing. Deep down I didn't want to do it. I wondered what would happen if I did the opposite from everyone else. I was tempted to be rebellious, but I didn't. There was something about the way it was done that made me automatically follow the crowd, I was a little disappointed with myself. The boys were brought in; their expressions hadn't changed from the day before, and again they didn't look at anyone in the court except the three judges. Their parents and guardians were like mere spectators.

The female judge continued in her role as the main speaker. After once again confirming with the boys that they understood the court's procedures she began her major speech.

'Together you have taken the life of an innocent man, a hard-working, well-respected teacher, who was doing you no harm. We have before us many accounts of how you committed this most hideous crime, but we know not why. Your lack of cooperation when questioned, and your inability to show any remorse, leaves us in no doubt whatsoever that you would commit this, or a crime of a similar nature, in the future. My experience, and the experience of my colleagues here on the bench, tells us that those who kill without motive are those who are most likely to kill again. We have looked at the reports brought before us, which include social services reports, school reports, and police reports, and although much of your behaviour may be deemed odd, you are both of sound mind. In other words you knew exactly what you were doing. We are here to work in the interest of the public, and to protect the public from people like you. And that is what we must do when considering our sentence. Do you have anything that you would like to say?'

The boys stayed silent. The judge repeated herself.

'Do you have anything to say?'

The boys said nothing.

'Lionel Ferrier. You have pleaded guilty to the murder of Mr Edgar Arnold Joseph. The sentence that I pass upon you is that you should be detained at Her Majesty's Pleasure, in such a place and under such conditions as the Secretary of State may now decide. You will be securely detained until the Home Secretary is satisfied that you have matured and are fully rehabilitated. You will only be granted liberty when the Home Secretary believes that you are no longer a danger to the public. Do you understand the sentence?'

For the first time Lionel looked uneasy. He looked around the room as if looking for his mum, and then he looked back to the judge.

'Yes. I know it means life, doesn't it?'

The judge took her glasses off and placed them on the table in front of her. She leaned forward, and the tone of her voice changed. She sounded gentler.

'Young man, you have to understand that this can be longer than life. A typical life sentence is in fact fifteen years; you could be detained for the rest of your natural life. It depends on your behaviour and the success or not of your rehabilitation. I suggest you talk to your legal representative, who will explain. But be in no doubt, however you look at it, you are going to be away for a long time.'

She turned to Ramzi.

'Ramzi Sanchin. You have pleaded guilty to conspiring to murder Mr Edgar Arnold Joseph. The sentence that I pass upon you is that you should be securely detained for ten years. Do you understand the sentence?'

'Yes,' replied Ramzi very quietly. 'I do understand.'

The judge put her glasses back on and made some notes, then she looked up and addressed the people in the public gallery.

'While this case has been going through the courts we have ordered that the names of these two young people be kept out of the public domain. This restriction was put in place in order to avoid any prejudgement by the press and others, and to respect the basic principle of law that states that every citizen is innocent until proven guilty. This principle is at the forefront of our minds when dealing with all cases, but even more so when dealing with juveniles in a case that has attracted a lot of media attention. We cannot allow our schools to become places of violence; young people must know that if they take dangerous weapons into schools they will be severely punished. And young people who kill innocent people should also know that the law will not protect them. And so this court will lift the restrictions on the publication of the names of the two defendants.'

She turned to Ramzi and Lionel.

'From here you will be taken to a secure unit to begin your sentences. I sincerely hope you are able to turn your lives around.' She then turned to the court security. 'Take them away.'

As we were leaving the courtroom Miss Ferrier walked past us at speed with her hands covering her face. I wanted to say something to her but it felt like the wrong time. Mrs Joseph was stopped by one of the solicitors representing the Crown. I could tell by the way they greeted each other that they had met before, and his smile and the tone of his voice told me that this was a man who was feeling victorious.

'Mrs Joseph. We have had several requests from members of the press for a statement from you.'

'No,' replied Mrs Joseph. 'I have nothing to say, and what good would it do, anyway?'

'You only need to go up there, say a few words, and they all run away to get their stories in. At the very least it clears the pavement,' the solicitor said smoothly.

I intervened. 'I think you should do it, Mrs Joseph. It will get rid of them and stop them from making things up.'

'But Jackson, what am I going to say to them?'

'Look,' said the solicitor. 'All you have to do is go out there and say you're glad it's all over, and that you just want to get on with your life. That's all.'

She seeked reassurance. 'Is that really all?'

'That's all,' he said.

'OK, I'll do it.'

We headed out and when we got outside the press were standing in a semi-circle, as if waiting for her arrival.

'Now, Mrs Joseph,' said the solicitor. 'Remember, say as little as you like, just don't get pulled into answering their questions. Remember that all-important phrase, no comment.'

Mrs Joseph stood on the steps in front of the court and waited awkwardly for a while as the cameras flashed. Then she began to speak.

'This has been a very difficult time for me, and it has been a difficult time for everyone at Marston Hall school. I can't speak for everyone at the school, but I can say that I am glad this is over. I have never wanted revenge, and I have never made any personal judgements about anyone involved in this case. We are all victims of something. I know it won't be easy, but as much as I can I would like to put this episode behind me and get on with the rest of my life without my much-loved husband, who I miss every day. Thank you.'

Someone shouted from the crowd, 'In your opinion, how long do you think the murderers should serve?'

'No comment,' she replied.

Someone else shouted, 'Do you think that schools should tighten their security? Would metal detectors be useful?'

'No comment.'

Then someone else shouted, 'Do you plan to re-marry?'

Well, she didn't like that.

'How dare you ask me such a question at a time like this? How dare you ask me that question at all? If you want to cover this story that's one thing, but you have no right at all to ask me questions of that nature. You should be ashamed of yourself, and if you're not you should go back to your school of journalism and learn some manner and some ethics.'

I clapped, but I was the only one who did. The other reporters just turned and left, presumably to submit their articles.

CHAPTER 17

The Family Extension

Mrs Joseph and I left the court and went back to the restaurant in the park for lunch. We reviewed the morning's events, our main topic of conversation being the lifting of the restrictions to name the boys and how this could make life harder for Miss Ferrier.

After we parted I went to the library where I went on the internet and skimmed through a few books, looking at this whole idea of being detained at Her Majesty's Pleasure. I thought it was a strange use of the word pleasure, and a very strange sentence indeed. I found that some people who had received this sentence had been released in a year, whilst others had spent over twenty years inside. It was believed that there were some people who would never be released. I thought of it as a non-sentence. It was like saying, look, we have a bag of sentences, but we don't know which one is for you, so we'll just keep you locked up until we've worked it out. In the silence of that library I thought hard about Lionel or Ramzi, and I couldn't decide who I thought had received the worst sentence.

The media works quickly, that's for sure. By the time I had arrived home my mum was sitting on the living-room floor reading the *City News* and some other evening newspapers. She handed me one.

'Read that,' she said.

I began to read the article. It started by explaining the sentences that were handed out but then focused on the speech that Mrs Joseph made outside the court. The article ended by saying, 'After making the statement Mrs Joseph left with her son.'

The moment I'd finished reading my mum spoke her mischievous mind.

'So, you've extended the family now. You didn't tell me that you had another mother.'

'Don't believe everything you read in the papers,' I replied.

'So what was it like?' she said very seriously.

I pointed to the newspapers.

'It was probably nothing like it says in those. It was spooky. Lionel's and Ramzi's foster parents just held their heads down as if they were at a funeral, and Lionel and Ramzi hardly said a thing again, it was as if they were in another world. They were like zombies. And then on our way out this reporter asked Mrs Joseph if she planned to re-marry, and I'm telling you Mum, she went ballistic. It's the first time I'd ever seen her lose it like that. She was angry boy.'

'I don't mind, you know,' my mother said as if to change the subject. I had no idea what she was on about.

'You don't mind what?' I asked, trying to tease more out of her.

'I don't mind if you have another mother. You know me, open-minded, willing to try anything. So two mums it is, then?'

'Yeah, two mums to make up for no dad.'

My mum looked at me awkwardly, then she looked down towards the floor.

'Well, two mums are a lot better than two dads, I can tell you,' she said.

'Can you?'

'Yes, for you anyway. If you had two dads you would have a house of three males and you'd just be another male. A younger one maybe, but still you'd be just another male. Now if you had two mums you'd be the only male, that would make you special. Think about it.'

It made a bit of sense, but only a bit.

'Mum, that's all well and good, but what would happen when something goes wrong?'

'What do you mean?'

'You know, when something goes wrong and you start blaming men for everything, I'd get it all, and I'd have no back up.'

'But think of it, you could just sit back and be spoilt. We would only bother you if we needed some maintenance jobs around the house.' She stood up quickly and headed for the kitchen. 'That's it. I've got an idea.'

'Yeah, food. That's a great idea,' I said.

'No. Why don't you invite your other mother round for dinner or something?'

Now this was a surprise, my mother rarely invited people around for meals. I thought it was either a joke or she was up to something.

'What, so you can gang up on me?

'No, serious,' she said seriously. 'Invite her round. You keep going on about her, you spend so much time with her, and you say I shouldn't believe what I read in the papers, so invite her round. I only spoke to her for a short time but she sounded nice on the phone.'

'OK,' I said. 'I will. But don't blame me if it all goes wrong. And no fighting over me. Now, what's for dinner?'

CHAPTER 18

Very Bleak House

I liked the idea of having Mrs Joseph round for dinner, but then I also liked the idea of two mums. So for a couple of days I had mad thoughts about what two mums could mean. I also read all the newspapers my mother bought. Then it was Sunday – the day I planned to go and see Miss Ferrier.

I left home nice and early and took a slow walk to Fentham Road. I arrived at the road at exactly nine o'clock, and Miss Ferrier was right, the road was quiet. No music playing, no dogs barking. I rang the bell at number thirty-five and stood well back, looking up, hoping for no change in the weather. Miss Ferrier opened the door and she was as nice as my mother.

'Hello. Good to see a young man who's on time. Come on in.'

From what I could see the house looked pretty normal, but she led me straight upstairs and into the front bedroom. It turned out that although the front bedroom had a bed in it, it also had a television, and a three-piece suite, and all the things you'd expect to find in a living room. She pointed to one of the chairs.

'Park yourself down there.'

I did as I was told.

'What's your name again?' she asked.

'Jackson. Jackson Jones.'

'That's right, Jackson Jones. So, what is it that you want to talk to me so much about, young Mr Jones?'

It was difficult to know where to start.

'First I'd just like to say I'm sorry about what happened to Lionel.'

She was quick to respond. 'What do you mean, sorry? He did the crime, so now he'll do the time.'

'But it's still sad, and it must be hard for you.'

'Who cares about me? I've had people telling me that I'm a bad mother, I've been investigated by welfare people, I've had people throw things at me in the streets, even my own son's told me that I'm born evil, so who really cares if it's hard for me?'

'I do.'

She paused to laugh. 'Rubbish. What do you know about me? You're just a boy. I have a pain in my foot that's older than you.'

'I can't feel your pain but that doesn't mean that I haven't got any feelings.'

She began to stare at me and I thought she was going to tell me to get out. She clapped her hands and rubbed them together.

'Do you want a cup of tea, then?'

Relieved I replied, 'No thanks, I had a big breakfast. Miss Ferrier, can you tell me, was Lionel always as quiet as he was in school?'

'Do you mean was he always strange? Let me tell you, Lionel was the best baby a mother could have. I mean that. I won't go into details, that's woman's talk, but even his birth was a pleasure. Whatever people call normal, that's what he was. When he was small he used to be way ahead of the rest of his class, and you couldn't stop him talking.' She paused for a moment. 'His dad should have been given the sentence he got.'

'It sounds like he was a great kid, you really loved him.'

'I was a proud mother,' she said, 'proud of my son.'

'I hope you don't mind me asking,' I continued, 'I mean, you can tell me to shut up, but where is his dad?'

'I don't know. One day he left. No, that's not right. One day I kicked him out. I had to. He started collecting guns and knives and playing with them as if they were toys. One day I'm sitting in here and he comes in carrying a dead cat, can you believe that, the man had found a cat that had been run over. He takes it round the back garden and begins to take the thing apart. Not only that, he gets Lionel and makes him watch it all. Can you imagine being nine years old and watching your father tearing a cat apart? And he did it more than once. He had all kinds of animals in here, and most of them he killed himself.'

I began to see a link between Lionel's behaviour and his dad's but I couldn't understand why his dad started acting like that. When I asked Miss Ferrier she didn't know either. But then she told me that one day it just stopped.

'Just like that?' I asked.

'Yes, just like that. He stopped killing animals but he started beating me. Just like that. Now you must understand, this man took no drugs, he didn't drink, well, a social drink every now and then, you know, but he was never drunk, and his parents loved him.'

'So why did he start doing all this crazy stuff?'

She headed for the door. 'I have no idea. Are you sure you don't want a cup of tea?

'No, I'm fine, thanks.'

She went to make herself some tea and I did some more thinking. By the time she came back I had many more questions to ask but I suspected that her good-will wasn't going to last much longer. She came back with a photo album that she handed to me.

'Look at those,' she said.

She began to sip her tea; I began to look through the album. Every photo was a photo of Lionel. Lionel just after birth, Lionel in the hospital cot, Lionel on his potty, Lionel taking his first steps, Lionel on his first bike, Lionel at a theme park, Lionel with the girl next door. It was the Lionel Ferrier picture show. Some of the photos featured his parents, but most were of him alone.

After I had a good look I handed back the album and said, 'That wasn't so long ago, really, was it?'

'No, that's right, it seems like yesterday, but then he lost the plot, just like his father. They both just lost the plot. Let me show you something else.'

She held the waist of her skirt down and carefully lifted her blouse up a couple of centimetres, just enough for me to see three lines of stitched wounds.

'That's what his father did to me, and there's more on my back and arms. I'm telling you I was so close to death that I could see my ancestors. He came in one day and told me that I was getting in the way of his spirit and messing up his vibes so I had to go, and then he started stabbing me. Lionel just sat there as if he was watching a cat being cut up.'

I was truly shocked. 'Gosh. I'm so sorry, Miss Ferrier.'

'I don't want to scare you but this is reality, this is what happened, and you're only getting a bit of it. All those people out there who make judgements don't know a thing, they just read stuff in the papers or hear rumours and they believe anything.' As she continued she began to cry. 'If anyone knew the pain that I've been through they wouldn't be so quick to judge. I almost died in this house, I almost bled to death and all my so-called partner and son could do was stand over me and watch. If it weren't for a neighbour who heard us struggling I wouldn't be here now. So I kicked him out. Then Lionel took over. He didn't stab me but he thinks that it's his duty to run the house, so what does he do, he runs the house just like his dad did. Look at me. I live in this room, I live in a bedsit in my own house, because Lionel wants the house to himself and he doesn't want to see me unless he wants something from me. What kind of life is this for a grown woman? What did I ever do to anyone to deserve this? I'm sorry. I've said too much.'

Still clutching the photo album she went over to a bedside table and took some tissues out of a box.

'I'm really sorry. I bet you weren't expecting this. You'll be having nightmares. And I'm sorry about drenching you the other day. You want to see the grief I get from the kids around here, it's the only way to keep them away. They think I'm mad, but it's my way of staying sane. I'm not an evil woman.'

'I know, Miss Ferrier. I don't believe everything I hear, and that's why I'm here. I want to get to the bottom of this.'

'But I just don't understand why it's so important to you. What are you after?' she asked.

'I was in the playground when Lionel stabbed the teacher. What I saw that day was horrible, and I just can't stop thinking about it. I'm not sure if I'm really

103

over it yet, but I just know there's more to it than what I saw. Why would Lionel or Ramzi take a knife to school?'

'I don't know. Lionel did strange things with knives but I've never known him to take one to school, and if he did it wasn't one from this house.'

I felt it was time for me to leave but I had one more question.

'How well do you know Ramzi, Lionel's friend?'

'I didn't know him at all,' she replied to my surprise. 'One day Lionel came home and said he had another servant. When I asked him what he meant he just said, you're my servant, and now he has another one. One at home, one at school. And that's all he said. The first time I ever saw that Ramzi boy was in court.'

'You mean he'd never come here?'

'Oh yes, he'd come here, but any time he came Lionel made me stay in my room. He said he was ashamed of me.'

I was shocked, but I didn't want her to see that. I thought I should show her kindness. I stood up. 'Miss Ferrier, thanks for talking to me, I really mean that. I have never thought you were mad or wicked or anything like that. Even when you wet me up.'

'I'm sorry, but I thought you were like all the others.'

'I understand, Miss Ferrier. Are you going to tell

Lionel that I visited you?'

She threw the photo album down on to the chair I had been sitting on.

'No. He's told me never to write to him, never to visit him. He even told me never to speak about him. You see what my life is like. It doesn't get any worse.'

I said goodbye, left the house, turned right and ran for my life. The gang were much slower than before, but now I knew that they took to the street about ten-thirty on Sundays. This kind of knowledge could save my teeth.

CHAPTER 19

The Big Match

When I arrived home that morning after visiting Miss Ferrier I knew that I could have stopped my investigations on that day. I had proved myself right to myself, and I had nothing to prove to anyone else. There were reasons for Lionel and Ramzi's madness. Lionel was bad all right, but I had found out why he was bad. I knew that it wouldn't be right to blame everything on his father but his father did have a lot to do with the way that Lionel viewed the world, and the way he saw life, and death. Just like Miss Ferrier said, I tried to imagine what I would have been like if I had known my dad and he had dismembered animals in front of me, and did all the other things that he had in front of Lionel, but it was impossible to imagine. You'd never know how these kinds of things would affect you until they actually happened to you, and these are things that you would never want to happen to you. Although I only had my mother to raise me I did have a stable home, so trying to think what life was like for Ramzi was also impossible. I couldn't imagine what it would be like to not only move home, but to change parents once a year. How do you collect things, how do you keep up with hobbies and things like that? I was of the belief that Ramzi had so little control over his life that he was easy to control. Anyone could have led him, and they could have led him anywhere.

So Lionel and Ramzi were corrupted kids, they had raw deals in life, they were loners, they were weirdoes. That pretty much explained their actions. They lived in a crazy world and so they did some crazy things. Things were falling into place and I was feeling a little better knowing that I was right; it wasn't as simple as it seemed. My therapy was working, but the questions kept coming. Why did they bring a knife to school? As bad as they were I wouldn't have thought they wanted to start cutting up animals in the playground. What made them turn on Mr Joseph? As bad as they were they had never launched unprovoked attacks on people before. Why Mr Joseph, what had he done? I still had more work to do.

I told my mum what I had found out and how I was feeling about it all, and believing that it was all over she congratulated me on what she called my 'first case'. She didn't say much else. I had been hoping that it may get her to speak about my dad for a bit. She never really talked about him, and over the years

I had gathered only random facts about him. She said he was just passing through; she didn't hate him; she never told me what he looked like; she said she had three names for him and she really didn't know which one was his real name. I used to think he was a gangster, or a secret agent who was only known by a code name. When I asked my mum after telling her about 'my case' if he would have done anything like what Lionel's dad did, she said, 'No, that was part of the problem, he did nothing, absolutely nothing.'

I felt frustrated not knowing who my father was, but the truth was that my mother didn't really know who my father was either. But I had the feeling that one of my future cases was going to be about me. Maybe one day I could use my investigative skills to track down my father. Maybe.

I did nothing but enjoy the rest of the summer holiday for a couple of weeks. I read a couple of books, listened to some music, saw a couple of films, I even went skiing on an artificial ski slope a few times, but it was as if I was trying to hide from reality. I had a greater calling. I had to get back on the case. So my next step was to take up my mother's suggestion. Sometimes my mother could be very sarcastic, she would say things that she didn't really mean, so one evening I asked her how serious she was about me inviting Mrs Joseph round for dinner.

'Deadly serious,' she replied. 'I've never been more serious in my life.'

'Why are you so keen on meeting her?' I asked.

'I'm just a responsible mother, and it's good to know the company your son is keeping. I've spoken to her on the phone but I think it's my duty to see her in the flesh. If my son is spending so much time with a woman I think it's only right that I should meet her,' she said with a smile.

I had not seen Mrs Joseph for some time and I wanted to tell her about my meeting with Miss Ferrier, but when I called her she didn't answer her phones. I was getting concerned, in a way she was the best friend I had and I wanted to keep her informed. When I finally got her on the phone she told me she had gone to the countryside to take a break. She stayed in a little family-run hotel by a stream and she said it did her a world of good. I thought it would be good if we could meet up. As always she was happy to meet me.

'I want to take you to a big match,' she said. 'Meet me on Saturday afternoon, at four, outside the town hall.'

I was intrigued. 'So what's this big match, then? You don't have swimming matches, so is it netball, basketball, boxing? Hey, you not taking me to a boxing match, are you?'

She laughed down the phone.

'You'll see. All I'll say now is that you'll be thrilled.'

Saturday was only two days away and I thought the right thing to do was to wait and see what she had in store, but I couldn't do the right thing. I watched the local TV sports news to see what was happening in the area that week but found nothing. I searched the newspapers trying to find news of any games but found nothing. All my detective skills got me nowhere. So when I met her on Saturday afternoon I felt at a slight disadvantage not knowing our final destination. I looked down the road, looking for clues, and asked, 'So where're we going, then?'

'In there,' she said, pointing at the town hall. 'That's the venue.'

'It *is* boxing,' I said, knowing that some boxing matches had been held there in the past.

'No,' she said. 'Come on in.'

The town hall was a large old place, often used for weddings and dances. As we went in she stopped and looked at a wall that was covered with posters advertising various events.

'That's us,' she said, pointing to a poster. 'That's what we're going to.'

It was a chess match.

'It starts in an hour and a half,' she continued. 'Plenty of time to get a drink and unwind. You have to be in a particular state of mind to play or watch a chess match.'

I reached for my high-pitched voice.

'A chess match. Who goes out and watches a chess match on a Saturday afternoon? It's so un-cool.'

'We do.'

'Do we?'

'Yes we do. Come on, I'll buy you a drink.'

We went to the café on the first floor and I began to tell her about my meeting with Miss Ferrier. She listened as I tried to recall every word of our conversation, and how I felt at the time.

'I knew it,' she said. 'Obviously I didn't know all of that but I knew that something like this must have gone on, I just didn't know it was that bad. Now you can see why Lionel and Ramzi go together, they needed each other. They were both very unhappy at home, both lacked older role models. When Ramzi was being moved around so much he wouldn't have time to build up relationships with his foster parents, male or female, and if Lionel's dad was so twisted and his mother was virtually kept prisoner in her room, what kind of a relationship could he build with them? When they heard other kids at school talking about their mums and dads what would they have to say? Nothing.'

I felt I had to defend broken families.

'But just because they come from broken families that doesn't mean they automatically end up evil. I come from a broken family.'

Mrs Joseph expanded her theory. 'There are very few perfect families, most families are broken in one way or another, but let's be honest, these two come from really broken families. Even so, if a family is really broken, I mean really really broken, kids can still do well if they are shown love. That's the important thing. It doesn't matter what shape or size your family is, if you feel loved and cared for you can deal with life, but they weren't loved! These two came from very unstable, unpredictable homes, so they felt unwanted. When they went to school they didn't fit in with the rest, so they hung out together.'

'Yeah,' I said. 'That makes sense, and I think Lionel got his ideas of controlling people from his father, and Ramzi was easily led, and easy to control.'

'That's right. And even though he was being controlled, for him it was the only friendship he had. That's why they needed each other. One needed to lead and one needed to be led. And they were both outsiders. Drink up and let's go.'

The chess spectators began to fill the café. An odd bunch they were, a real mix of people. Lots of men wearing caps, lots of women with spectacles hanging around their necks, and lots of men and women who looked suspiciously like teachers trying not to look like teachers. Then there were young kids who for some reason were wearing their school uniforms, and other school kids trying desperately not to look like school kids. And they were all so well behaved. As they started to head for the hall I popped the question to her. As soon as I started speaking I realised I should have rehearsed it.

'I was wondering, Mrs Joseph, well, we were wondering, you know, me and my mum were both wondering if you could, if you would like to – feel free to say no – we were wondering if you would like to come to our house and have dinner one night. Like I said, you don't have to, I mean you don't have to say yes to be polite. If you think it's a bad idea that's cool, it's just that me and my mum, we thought it would be, you know – nice.'

It was hard work, but she smiled and said, 'Yes.' Without hesitation. 'When?'

'Well,' and now I hesitated. I hadn't really thought this through. 'We go back to school the week after next, so maybe before we go back. How about some time next week. If that's too soon just say so.'

'I will, and it's not too soon. Next week is fine. How about Friday? That way we can have a big build-up.'

'Why the big build-up?' I asked, looking as confused as I sounded.

'Well, you seem so nervous. A big build-up will give you more time to be nervous. Why are you so nervous, are you doing the cooking or something?'

'No,' I replied quickly. 'I may help with the

cooking, but I couldn't do it all. The invitation was my mum's idea originally, and I just thought you may not be up for it.'

'So is it Friday, then?' she asked.

'Yes. Aren't you going to write it down?'

'No,' she said, smiling, I'll remember it.'

'Great. About six?'

'Six is fine.'

'Nice,' I said. 'I'm sure it will be OK. 'I'll double-check with my mum and let you know tomorrow, but I'm sure it's cool.'

She turned off her phone. 'Come on, we don't want to miss the start of the match now.'

She handed me a ticket and we went to see the action.

CHAPTER 20

Double Dating

I never want to go to a chess match again, or maybe not until I've learnt how to play. I wouldn't say it was like watching paint dry, it was more like watching paint being made. I knew there was something happening and maybe it had a purpose, but I just didn't get it, and even if I were able to get it I'm not sure if I would spend money and an evening getting more of it. I found watching two people thinking very strange, and I'm sure it can't be called a sport when the only movement is when they raise their hands to move the pieces. The only other movement was when someone was eliminated and they walked off, or when opponents changed seats. I didn't like it and I told Mrs Joseph that, but she told me that one day I would change my mind. She also told me that she was looking forward to Friday, so that allowed me to call the evening a success.

When I arrived home Mum was still up reading a newspaper. She was pleased that Mrs Joseph was happy to visit us that Friday but not very pleased with what I had to say next.

'Mum, you know on Friday when Mrs Joseph comes, I'd like to invite someone else. I'd like to invite Miss Ferrier.'

She threw the newspaper down.

'Are you crazy? Are you out of your mind? You've invited Mrs Joseph over for dinner and you expect her to sit at the same table as the mother of the boy who killed her husband. You're mad, absolutely mad. I would get that one right out of your head, put that idea in the bin straight away.'

I was sure she was overreacting.

'Mum, it's not as crazy as it sounds. Miss Ferrier is no monster and anyway I'm sure that Mrs Joseph is not going to judge her by the actions of her son. I mean, how would you like it if you were judged by my actions?'

'God forbid.'

'There you go. You see, Mrs Joseph is really reasonable, she's not going to fall for that trap, one thing she does for sure is think for herself.'

Mum went to the kitchen and started to shout at me as she made herself a hot drink.

'Forget it, Jackson, it's not going to happen. I think you've got this one completely wrong. As far as this case goes I think so far so good, but don't go too far, because that's no good, and people may get hurt. I don't think Miss Ferrier would want to come anyway.'

'I'm going to ask her,' I said.

'You know I like you to make your own decisions and take responsibility for them,' my mum said. 'But I think you're asking for trouble this time. Mrs Joseph may seem easy-going and all that, but that could just be a front, she could be hurting up inside and putting on a brave face, and bringing her face to face with the mother of her husband's killer could make her really emotional, Jackson. I'm not sure about it. Be careful.'

'How about if I ask Mrs Joseph first? If Mrs Joseph's cool with it then I'll ask Miss Ferrier.' I was determined to convince my mum.

She came back into the room and sat back on her seat, holding her mug of tea with both hands.

'I don't see the point,' she said eventually.

'I do,' I said. 'Miss Ferrier has done nothing to Mrs Joseph and Mrs Joseph knows that. Mrs Joseph is a very compassionate and caring woman, and if she knew all that Miss Ferrier has been through she would be the first to show her some understanding. She wouldn't think of her as a horrible woman like some people do. And if Miss Ferrier knew Mrs Joseph, she would probably really look up to her. She needs to see strong positive women, she needs role models. If they decide to meet not much can go wrong. If they don't get on with each other they'll just say goodnight and that's it, but if they do get on it will be a great example of how good can come from bad.'

'You've got it all worked out,' said my mother. 'And how's this going to help your case? I thought your case was finished. Closed?'

'No, I haven't got it all worked out. I have a lot worked out but like any good detective I'm always looking for clues. And anyway, it may help, you know, bringing people together. I think I still have some way to go.'

The next day I rang Mrs Joseph and put the idea to her.

'Mrs Joseph, you know you're coming to our house on Friday?'

'Yes.'

'Well, I had this idea.'

'Yes.'

'If you think it's a stupid idea just tell me.'

'Yes.'

'It's just an idea, right?'

'Yes.'

'Well, would you mind if I invited Miss Ferrier round as well?'

There was a long silence. Then when Mrs Joseph spoke she spoke very slowly.

'Do you mean Lionel's mum?'

'Yes,' I said very, very nervously.

There was a long silence. I could hear her thinking.

And then the phone went dead. I couldn't believe it; she had put the phone down on me. I had managed to upset my detective partner, I had lost her confidence and friendship. I wanted to call her back and apologise but I wasn't sure if that would make things worse. I wanted to tell my mother but I could hear her saying 'I told you so'. I sat still, trying to imagine how she was feeling and getting angry with myself for going over the line. An hour after she put the phone down on me my phone rang. I could see on the display that it was Mrs Joseph and for a moment I thought that maybe I shouldn't answer it. I wasn't sure if I could take a telling-off from her, but I also thought it would be disrespectful if I ignored her. I answered.

'Hello.'

'Hello, Jackson. It's me, Mary, Mrs Joseph.'

'Hi, I'm really sorry, it was a stupid idea.'

'Don't be sorry, and it wasn't a stupid idea. I'm just going through a rough time at the moment and it took me by surprise. It would have been our wedding anniversary today. That kind of thing brings back lots of memories.'

I struggled to find something else to say. Simply saying, 'I'm very sorry, Mrs Joseph,' didn't feel adequate. But that was all I could say.

Mrs Joseph continued, 'I have thought about it. At first it did sound rather crazy, but now I have to say that I think it's something I would like to do.'

I was liberated from my despair. I wanted to share my relief with her, but I held back.

'I haven't asked Miss Ferrier yet. I wanted to talk to you first, but I will talk to her today.'

'Well, you do that, Jackson, and tell her I would be happy to meet her. What about your mum, what does she think about it?'

'She's cool,' I replied. 'She wasn't sure if it was a good idea at first, a bit like you, but she said I should take responsibility for my own decisions. She's that kind of a mum.'

'I'm looking forward to meeting her. She sounded really nice on the phone.'

I was making progress, but I had to speak to Miss Ferrier, and having no phone number for her meant I had to go to her house. I wasted no time and went straight away. The problem was by the time I reached Fentham Road it was two p.m. and the street was full of activity. Children were running wild, dogs were barking loudly and running wild, and the music was even louder. I tucked my chin in and began to walk down the road but it wasn't long before someone spotted me. I heard a girl shout. 'There's that boy from central.'

It felt as if everybody stopped what they were doing and started heading my way.

'I'm not from central,' I shouted.

'Get him,' shouted one boy.

So I ran straight ahead, but then I saw a group of kids that had spread themselves across the road to stop me. There was nowhere to go; I was going to get a kicking. Just then I heard someone call my name.

'Jackson, Jackson, come here.'

It was Carla.

'Hurry up. Come on.'

Her house was between me and the gang that was waiting ahead so I ran in there.

'Thanks, Carla,' I said gratefully. 'What is it about this street, and why do they think that I come from central?'

Carla closed the door behind me. 'Welcome back, Mr Jackson. It's so good to see you again. I really don't mind saving your life but I thought you learnt your lesson the last time you were down here.'

'I've got some unfinished business.'

She pointed to the door. 'They've got some unfinished business. It's called you.'

We were still standing in the hallway.

'But what's this central thing?' I asked.

'They've this gang that hang around in town. Any time the kids from here go to town they get chased by them, so if they see a new face around here and they think they come from central they go for them. The problem is now they think any stranger is from central. What are you doing around here again anyway?'

I knew she wasn't going to like my reply.

'I've come to see Miss Ferrier.'

'Who?'

'Miss Ferrier. Lionel Ferrier's mother, you know, at number thirty-five.'

Carla placed one hand firmly on her hip and pointed towards number thirty-five.

'What, you're going to see that weirdo down there, the murderer's mum?'

'I wouldn't have put it that way but I think we're taking about the same person.'

She turned and shouted upstairs.

'Jason. Do you remember that nice young boy Jackson?'

'Yeah,' came the shout back. 'I remember him, what about him?'

'He's here, and guess what, he's going down the road to see the mad woman, the murderer's mum.'

'It's none of your business, Carla,' shouted Jason.

'Ah, what do you know?' she shouted back. She then opened the door and signalled me out. 'Come on, I'll walk you down.'

'But you don't like her,' I said. 'You call her a murderer's mum and things like that, so why do you want to walk me down there?'

'Because if I walk with you the kids will leave you alone, but I'm not staying with you. I think that woman's evil, so you're going to have to make your own way out of here.'

I stepped out and she followed me. I felt quite secure as I walked down the road with her. No one attacked us physically but after a few metres we started to get the verbal. A girl who I recognised from my first trip down the street was the first. She walked behind us with a couple of her friends and began to talk to the back of our heads.

'So are you scared of being on your own, then, little boy? You can't protect him all the time, you know, Carla.'

'Shut up, Tasha.'

Tasha and her group backed off when we were approached by four boys from the front. Their spokesperson addressed me.

'You're going to get dropped.'

'Don't say anything,' said Carla.

A few other things were shouted but we just ignored them, and then we reached number thirty-five. Carla looked at me unimpressed.

'I think you're a nice boy, Jackson, but I really can't see what you want with someone like her. Apart from what her son's done she's such a horrible person, she's a bitch and she's a witch.'

'Come on, Carla,' I replied. 'Where did you get all that from?'

'We live here so we know. You are just passing through, but we see what she's like all the time. I have to go now. Maybe you can drop by and see us again, but not when you're coming to see the beast.'

She walked away and for a moment I stood and thought about Carla's hatred of Miss Ferrier, but then I saw that group of boys heading my way so I rang the bell.

Miss Ferrier shouted through the door again.

'Who is it?'

'Me, Jackson,' I said hurriedly. 'Can you open up quickly, please? There are some bad people coming my way.'

Fortunately she opened up quickly and I was soon inside. She took me upstairs to her living room, gave me that photo album again, and a small carton of fruit juice. I looked at the photo album and came across a photo of Lionel I hadn't seen before. He was smiling and I noticed that there was a hand on his shoulder but the photo had been cut in half so I couldn't see whose hand it was.

'Lionel looks really happy here,' I said.

'Do you think so?' she replied.

'Yeah, I think so. But why is the photo cut in half?'

'Because his dad was standing next to him,' she said abruptly.

'So is that his dad's hand on his shoulder?'

'Yes, and the only reason he's smiling is because the photographer told him to. Look very carefully and you'll see it's a forced smile. Look at his eyes and you'll see his eyes don't match his face.'

I looked, and she was right. His eyes stared beyond the camera and his smile looked as if it was fixed on. His lips were in the right position but his face wasn't smiling. Miss Ferrier stared at the photo album in my hand and began to speak.

'Sometimes I look at those photos and wonder what Lionel would have been like if his life was different. Did I just get involved with the wrong type of man? Was I a bad mother? I don't know. I just wish that I could have a normal son. I really want to see him but I'm scared to go, I'm scared of how he will react if I go to see him. It could make things worse between us.'

'Do you miss him?' I asked.

'I think about him all the time, and I can't get used to the absolute silence in the house now that he has gone, but I'd rather have silence than violence. I haven't had peace in my life for a long time, but now that I have some peace and some freedom I don't know what to do with it. All I do is sit here thinking about what life would be like if things were different. I feel happiest when I'm dreaming about how life could have been. I hardly ever go out and I have no friends. It's not much of a life, but at least I have some peace now. I don't know what will happen to Lionel. I just hope that somehow he turns into a better person, but I just don't think it will happen.'

Miss Ferrier stopped speaking. Now was the time to ask her the big question, but I was nervous.

'Miss Ferrier, you've told me what some people think of you and you know I don't agree with that rubbish, right?'

'Right.'

'And you know that I don't judge people, right?'

'Right.'

'OK. Now that's agreed I want to ask you something. What are you doing the day after tomorrow?'

She thought for a while. 'I'll be doing what I do every Friday. Nothing. I'll be sitting here letting the world pass me by.'

'Do you want to come to my house for dinner on Friday?'

She didn't hesitate to answer.

'No.'

'Just no?' I said.

'That's right,' she said. 'Just no.'

'Why?'

'Why should I?'

'Just for a meal, just for a change of scenery. You just said you don't get out much.'

'No. I'm not going.'

'But why, Miss Ferrier, why not?'

'For a start I've never been to anyone's house for a meal, and anyway what good's a change of scenery?'

I began to plead.

126

'Please, Miss Ferrier, my mum said it's fine, and it will be good. I'll come and get you and make sure you come back safely –'

'You,' she interrupted. 'You can't even walk down this street safely.'

'Yes, but this street is different. Don't worry, I'll make sure everything is fine.'

Miss Ferrier lowered her head until her chin was resting on her chest. She was still for a while; it felt like a long while. She then raised her head and looked towards the ceiling for another long while, and then she looked at me, right into my eyes.

'OK. If you promise to look after me.'

'Great. I promise,' I said, raising my clenched fist in front of my face, but then I realised I had forgotten something.

'Oh, Miss Ferrier, there's one more thing.'

'Don't tell me you're vegans,' she said, rolling her eyes.

'No,' I said. 'It's just that that Mrs Joseph is going to be there too.'

She stood up at the speed of lightning.

'Her? Are you mad? No way. Forget it.'

'Why not?' I found myself asking again.

'Why not? Come on, Jackson, I know you're young but you weren't born yesterday, use your common sense. Look what Lionel has done to her life. The poor woman has lost her husband, so I can't imagine what she thinks of me. She must hate me, she must hate my guts, she must hate every bone in my body.'

I tried to slow her down.

'No she doesn't. She didn't say anything to you when you were in court, did she? She's not like a lot of people. She's not out for revenge, she doesn't hold a grudge against you, and she knows that I've come here now to ask you.'

She looked back into my eyes, her voice dropped.

'You mean she knows you're here asking me now?'

'Yes.'

'And said she would eat at the same table as me?'

'Yes.'

'Why?'

'Because she's not judging you, because she's not blaming you.'

Miss Ferrier sat down and stared down into the half-empty cup of tea that she was holding tightly with both hands on her lap. The silence was so long that I found myself staring into the cup myself, as if the answer was in there somewhere. I began to notice the sounds of the birds outside, the dogs' barks got louder, as did the noise of the planes flying in the sky. After what felt like an hour she turned to me and said, 'Yes.'

CHAPTER 21

Night at the Round Table

When I woke up on Friday it felt as if Judgement Day had arrived. All the confidence that I had had was gone and I began to ask myself if bringing Mrs Joseph and Miss Ferrier together was such a good idea. I stayed in bed much longer than usual, but all I did was think negative thoughts about how it could all go tragically wrong, and when I started to picture Mrs Joseph leaning over the dinner table and plunging a knife into Miss Ferrier's heart I decided to get up.

My mother wasn't used to cooking for other people, she didn't like even like cooking for me much, so to give herself plenty of time to make mistakes she was up early reading recipes aloud as she moved around the kitchen. I tried to convince her that it would be fine to have what we ate normally, just more of it, but she wouldn't have it. It was a special occasion, so she had to make something special. I grabbed some fruit and got out of her way. She spent most of the day downstairs cooking and cleaning, and I spent most of it upstairs being nervous. It was difficult resisting the temptation to eat throughout the day with the smell of food constantly in the air, but I just kept telling myself I had to be hungry when they arrived. If it all went wrong at least I would have something to do – eat.

Mrs Joseph arrived right on time; when we opened the door for her she greeted us with open arms as if she was a long-lost relative.

'Hello, great to see you,' she said to my mother as they hugged hard. 'And you, Jackson, you handsome so and so, how are you?'

'I'm fine, just fine.'

'Come on in,' said my mother. 'It's really good to meet you in the flesh after all this time.'

They walked in, leaving me in the hall. I closed the door and went into the living room and felt rather guilty for interrupting them as they seemed to be getting on so well.

'Er . . . Mum, can I have some money?'

'What do you need money for?' she asked.

'For the minicab. I told Miss Ferrier that I would pick her up.'

My mum looked at Mrs Joseph. 'Are you really all right with this?'

Mrs Joseph didn't hesitate to reply. 'Yes, I am.'

'It's a pretty brave thing to do. I admire you,' said my mother.

'No, not at all,' said Mrs Joseph. 'I think she's the brave one, I'm just Little Miss Innocent, I'm not sure if I could do what she's doing if I were in her shoes.'

'You have a point,' said my mother. 'Now, Jackson, you need some money, do you?'

'Yes, Mum.'

'Well, you can't have any.'

'Mum, why?'

'Because you arranged all this, it's your project, so I think you should bear the cost. I was going to charge you for the food but I'll let you off with that,' my mum said playfully, 'but I still think that if you promised to transport your guest here then you should factor that into your costings. Basically, son, it's one of your expenses.'

'Oh, Mum,' I moaned.

'Don't moan,' she replied. 'You know what I told you, life is expensive and you have to learn to pay your way.'

'But, Mum, I've only got what I've saved up from my pocket money.'

'Good,' she said. 'So you can use that.'

So I had no choice. I called a minicab and used some of the money that I was saving up for a portable DVD player. It was much better viewing the kids on Fentham Road from the car. As we drove down the road I ducked my head to avoid being seen by them. When the car stopped I left the door open just in case

I needed a quick getaway and then I nervously rang the bell. It was as if Miss Ferrier was waiting by the door because the moment I rang the bell she opened it. She was dressed just as she was in court. She didn't say hello but she wasted no time in putting her questions to me.

'This is not such a good idea, is it? What's the point in all this? Why don't we just stop this now before it's too late?'

'Don't worry, Miss Ferrier,' I said, trying my best to reassure her and watch my back at the same time. 'Are you ready, can we go now?'

'If we must,' she replied.

We both sat on the back seat and she moaned all the way to my house. It wasn't nasty moaning, she wasn't being horrible or ungrateful, she just couldn't understand why anybody would want to be in her company. She probably wouldn't have admitted it, but I thought she was frightened.

When we arrived home she stopped moaning and began being as polite as she could. She followed me into the living room, where my mother and Mrs Joseph quickly stood up to greet her.

'This is my mother.'

They shook hands.

'Pleased to meet you.'

'Pleased to meet you.'

'And this is Mrs Joseph.'

They shook hands.

'Pleased to meet you.'

'Pleased to meet you.'

'Would you like a cup of tea?' my mother asked.

'No thanks,' replied Miss Ferrier.

'A drop of wine?'

'Wine?' said Miss Ferrier, a little surprised.

'Yes, wine. Red or white?'

'Actually, I've changed my mind. Can I have some tea, please?

'Yes of course,' said my mother, 'and you, Mary?'

'Yes please,' said Mrs Joseph.

'So it's Mary now, is it? I said.

'Do you have a problem with that?' my mother said as she headed for the kitchen.

We all sat down and Mrs Joseph, aka Mary, started with the small talk.

'So how was the taxi ride here?'

'It was OK,' replied Miss Ferrier. 'I haven't been in a cab for years, me.'

'You don't like them?' asked Mrs Joseph sympathetically.

'No, I've got nothing against them, it's just that I don't ever need one. Anything I want to do is within walking distance and if I have to venture further afield I use the bus. They get crowded sometimes, and if you get on one when the kids are coming home from school you'll be disgusted by the language they use, but I do like a bus ride every now and then. Do you use the buses?' she asked.

The talk until my mother returned to the room was about how buses had changed over the years. All I did was sit there and listen. It was quite interesting. I didn't know that buses used to have someone on them called a conductor who would go round and take fares and talk to people. And I didn't know that there used to be two number 35s, a 35a and a 35b. The 35a used to go all the way to the White Horse, but the 35b only used to go to the Royal Oak and turn back. I really didn't know that stuff. It was a strange thing to be talking about, I thought, but I think the only reason they were talking bus routes was because talking about why they were really together might be a bit more difficult.

When my mother returned the subject changed to matters more intellectual: the difference in prices between the various local supermarkets. It was all above my head. Just as that conversation was running out of steam my mother invited everyone into the dining room. Miss Ferrier and Mrs Joseph offered to help her bring the food to the table. I offered too and all I got was, 'It's all right, son, you just sit down and we'll bring the food to you. Besides, I can't risk any more broken plates.'

So when we sat down to eat the topic of conversation was set up.

Mrs Joseph went first. 'Well, Jackson, you've broken a few plates, then?'

'No, not a few. Two.' I replied.

'Come on, Jackson,' said my mother. 'Tell the truth.'

'Two,' I said.

'And yesterday?'

'That was you,' I said. 'I was passing the plate to you and it was you who dropped it.'

'I don't think so,' said my mother.

'I do,' I said.

'Jackson,' said Mrs Joseph. 'There's nothing wrong with dropping plates. I drop them all the time.'

Just then I noticed that Miss Ferrier was looking intensely at Mrs Joseph. Suddenly she stood up and spoke.

'I'm really sorry about what happened to your husband. I tried my best to raise my son to have good values but I wasn't the one that he listened to, I wasn't important to him. I'm really sorry, it wasn't my fault. You don't have to pretend that you like me, you know, I wouldn't blame you if you hated me, because if I was in your shoes I would be angry and I wouldn't be as calm as you. Just say what you want to me. Go on, say it, you don't have to be nice to me, and we don't need all this nice talk. Just say what you want to say.'

Mrs Joseph was as cool as anything. She smiled and said, 'Look, I'm not pretending, I'm not blaming you,

I'm not angry with you, and I'm not trying to be nice to you. Well, I am trying to be nice to you but only like I'm trying to be nice to Jackson, or his mum. Please relax, come on, sit down. Jackson thought we should all get together and we all agreed. There's no secret agenda. When I said I was pleased to meet you I really meant it.'

'You must hate me,' said Miss Ferrier.

'I don't,' said Mrs Joseph.

It was me who brought them together so I thought I should say something.

'No one's blaming you, Miss Ferrier, no one's angry with you, and no one's judging you. Trust me.'

'I trust you, Jackson,' said Miss Ferrier, looking into her food. 'I do trust you but this is all a bit strange to me. I can't understand why anybody would want to be in the same room as me.'

My mother joined in.

'Talk, that's what I say, communication. If we communicate we build up understanding, if we have understanding the world will be a better place.'

'That's right,' said Mrs Joseph. 'I agree with that. The world will be a better place if we all talked more and did a lot more exercise.'

Miss Ferrier jumped up and freaked out again.

'I've had enough of this. What do you want? What do you want? You didn't bring me here to just feed me, you didn't bring me here to talk about traffic, and supermarkets, and your communicating, and your exercise. Exercise? Who cares about exercise? You're up to something, I know it, you must be up to something.' She stood up and walked towards her coat.

'I'm going. I don't understand all this. I'm going.'

I knew that if I let her walk out I would probably never see her again, so I jumped up and pleaded with her.

'Honestly, Miss Ferrier, we're not up to anything, I can promise you that there's nothing going on. I just wanted you to meet my mum and meet Mrs Joseph. I did it because when you told me about the things that happened to you I could see you were not a bad mother, and I know that Mrs Joseph is not bitter, and I just thought that you both have something in common.'

'What do we have in common?' shouted Miss Ferrier.

'Well,' I said. 'Firstly, you're both very different from what most people may think.'

Miss Ferrier's voice was still raised. 'So if that's firstly what's secondly?'

'You are both women who have lost someone. In different ways of course, but you have both lost someone.'

She seemed to relax. She turned and sat back in her seat.

'Now,' said my mother, 'let's eat up.'

After that it was all good really. I felt a little left out because they talked about a lot of lady things, but it was all very civilised. At times they laughed together and at times they debated together. It was all so good that when I took Miss Ferrier home in the minicab we dropped Mrs Joseph off on the way. When we arrived at Fentham Road it was deserted. Miss Ferrier stepped out of the minicab and looked up at her house as if she had been away on holiday and was seeing it for the first time in a long time. She turned back to me.

'Thank you, Jackson.'

'It's OK,' I replied.

As she was about to shut the door she put her head in and said, 'Jackson, can I trust you?'

'Yes,' I said, 'You can trust me.'

She closed the door and the cab headed back home, and I felt an overwhelming sense of fulfilment and responsibility on my shoulders.

CHAPTER 22

Hostilities Increase

I returned to school two weeks later to find that nothing much had changed, except that I had to start preparing myself for my GCSE exams and the school had to start preparing itself to be inspected. Sounded like great fun. We have had some pretty negative reports before, and some good ones, but now there were lots of jokes going around about how this school report would read. Must do better, and stop stabbing teachers.

Maybe we weren't the best school in the world, but we weren't that bad, and most of the comments were lighthearted. Overall it was a pretty positive first day back considering what had happened last term, and just like Mrs Martel said in the morning assembly, we were a school looking to the future.

When l was leaving school I was looking to the future, I was certainly looking forward, but when I felt a slap across the back of my head it felt familiar. I turned round to see Terry Stock and his gang who had attacked me in the playground before. I wondered if they had a reason this time.

'You lot again,' I said. 'What's up?'

They didn't say anything but they looked a lot more serious than they did the last time. Then Terry raised both his hands and pushed me in the chest. I fell over and they gathered around me. The other boy kicked me and I heard someone shout 'fight'. This attracted the usual crowd, which I thought would work to my advantage, after all, the four of them wouldn't want to be seen beating up little helpless me. It turned out that they didn't mind at all, so when the four of them started kicking me on the ground I decided it was time for me to go. With the crowd trying to encourage me to fight back, I managed to stand up, put on a brave face, and run. They ran after me and the spectators ran after them, but my will to survive was much stronger than their will to see a fight, so I soon outran them. When they were out of sight I walked as quickly as I could in the direction of home but a couple of streets away I felt that now-familiar slap across the back of my head. It was them again; they had given up the chase so that they could intercept me on the way home.

'What's wrong with you lot?' I asked as calmly as I could. 'What have I done to hurt you?'

Terry tried to slap me in my face but I jerked my head back and he missed me. I was close though, I could smell the cheese and onion crisps on his hand.

'Why don't you just give it a rest?' he shouted.

'Give what a rest?' I said loudly.

'All your nosing around,' he said.

'Yeah, why don't you mind your own business?' said one of the girls.

'Yeah,' said Terry. 'Stop asking questions, will you?'

'I'm not hurting you,' I said.

The other boy spoke.

'You think you're really clever, don't you, you think you're someone special, don't you? Well you're not that special, and if you want us to show you why we'll show you now. I reckon we could knock you out in less than a minute. That would prove that you weren't very special, wouldn't it? Wouldn't it?' he shouted.

I was beginning to feel a bit worried now and I didn't mind showing it.

'It would,' I said.

'And you're not special, are you?' Terry said, now smiling wickedly.

'Not really.'

'Not really?' he said. 'You mean no, don't you? And I've heard that you've been speaking to Lionel Ferrier's mother.'

'What's wrong with that?

One of the girls started laughing.

'She's a witch,' she said.

'She's not a witch,' I said. 'She's nothing like a witch. People only say that because of Lionel, but she's so different to Lionel. I've spoken to her, she's even had dinner at my house and I can tell you she's no witch.'

'What, she had dinner at your house?' they all seemed to say at once.

'Yes,' I replied.

'You let that dirty woman into your home? What did you talk about?' asked one of the girls.

'Mind your own business,' I said.

Give him a kicking,' said the other girl.

Mr slaphappy Terry made another strike for me, I managed to avoid him again, and once more I did my favourite self-defence move. I ran.

I reached home safely; I knew I would because I was driven by fear and the desperate need to be somewhere safe, somewhere near my mother. But I was getting tired of running. I wasn't used to it, it wasn't like running for sport and I wasn't very good at it. Up until then I was the kind of school kid that had no enemies; OK I didn't exactly have a long list of friends either, I just wasn't important to other pupils or street gangs. Being mistaken as someone from central by the kids of Fentham Road was one thing, but I just didn't understand what Terry and his friends had against me. The more I thought about it the more scared I got, and it really was beginning to get to me. It was getting to me so much that I found it difficult to eat that night and I was becoming reluctant to go to school, and that was not like me. I was convinced that they would simply carry on from where they left off. Mum had noticed that I didn't eat much, so I pretended to be ill. I managed to fake it for two days and I could have lasted a few days more but I knew I had to do something, so I called her to my room. She knew that if I called her to the room something was wrong; she wasted no time in asking.

'What it is, Jackson?'

'I'm having some problems at school,' I said, looking down towards her feet.

'What is it? Has all this investigating you've been doing got you behind on your work?'

'No.'

'Is it something to do with Mrs Joseph and all that?'

'No.'

'What is it, then?'

I slowly raised my head to see her face but I couldn't speak whilst looking at her, so I lowered my gaze once again and then spoke.

'I'm being bullied.'

'You're being bullied?' she said with a smile that said she didn't quite believe me. 'You. Bullied. You love school, and you've only been back one day.'

I wasn't sure if I should have been angry because of her reaction or if I should explain. I gave her the benefit of the doubt and I began to explain.

'What happened was, last term I was in the playground and this group of kids came behind me and one of them slapped me in my head. Just like that. They threatened me and stuff and then they went off.'

The expression on her face changed, I could see she was beginning to be concerned. She came and sat next to me on my bed.

'That was last term,' she said.

'On Monday they got me outside the school and the same boy hit me again, then they chased me. I got away first but then they got me again.'

'But what were they doing it for?' Mum asked.

'I don't know.'

'What were they saying to you?'

'They were just saying silly things. They were just asking me if I thought I was a detective and calling me names. And they were calling Miss Ferrier a witch, but everyone does that. They're just bullies, and they're jealous because I'm doing something positive and they're just time wasters, and they want me to stop doing what I'm doing.'

'I think you're right,' said my mother. 'And you shouldn't let them do that. You know the rules about bullying; don't let them get away with it. You go to school tomorrow and tell the head teacher.'

Just then something strange happened. I could feel my body temperature rising. It started in the pit of my stomach and rose up, and as it rose it seemed to transport tears to the back of my eyes. I tried not to move, I felt as if any movement would release the tears and I could hear the little man in me saying, don't cry. My mother continued to speak.

'I'll write a note for you and you give it to Mrs Martel in the morning.'

I couldn't hold on any longer.

'No, Mum, I'm not going in on my own.' Once that first wave of tears was released my body just produced more and more, then my nose went warn and runny, and speaking and breathing at the same time became difficult.

'You have to come with me, Mum. Say if they're waiting at the gates, what do I do then? Next time they could do something really serious to me. I'm scared, Mum, really scared. If you come with me then Mrs Martel will know how serious this is. When I started to tell you at first you didn't take it that seriously, she probably won't.'

'I'm sorry, Jackson.' She put her arm around me. 'It's just because you're such a confident boy.'

'So?' I shouted and removed her arm from my shoulder. 'Does that mean confident boys don't get bullied?'

'I'm sorry,' she said, placing her arm back gently and rubbing my shoulder. 'I'm sorry. You're right. I'm going to school with you tomorrow and we'll sort this out.'

*　　*　　*

It's not cool to be seen going to school with your mother. The playground feels bigger, the corridors seem longer, and the kids look meaner, but it had to be done.

Mrs Martel was surprised to see us. Presuming that I had news about the case she asked, 'So what's new? I thought you had wrapped up your investigations.'

'It's not about my investigations,' I said, and then my mother took over.

'Mrs Martel, Jackson hasn't been to school for the last couple of days because he's being bullied. I've never seen him so frightened, he wouldn't have come in today if I wasn't with him, and I can't let him come back if something isn't done about it.'

'Is this true, Jackson?' said Mrs Martel, and this made me think, why is it that the first reaction from adults is to doubt you when you tell them you've been bullied?

'Yes. It's true.'

'And who's doing the bullying?' she asked.

'Terry Stock and his gang. I don't know their names, another boy and two girls.'

'And you don't know their names?' asked Mrs Martel again. Now my mother was beginning to feel how I felt. She got angry.

'He just told you, didn't he? He said he knows one of them but he doesn't know who the others are.

146

What do you want, names, addresses and dates of birth? Come on, he's doing his best.'

'I understand,' said Mrs Martel. 'But you must understand we have to correctly identify the culprits before we can do anything. I know it's a difficult time for you both but if we make mistakes it only makes thing worse.'

'Just do something,' said my mother. 'Or I'm taking him home.'

It was good to see my mother sticking up for me. She was always so laid-back until she found that laid-back wasn't working for her, then she turned into a do-it-now-before-it-does-you type of person. But I was also beginning to see Mrs Martel's approach. She turned to me.

'If we went into the playground now, Jackson, could you identify the other three?'

I knew I could. 'Yes.' But I didn't want to. 'But I really don't want to. Do you know Warren Stanmore, miss?'

'Yes.'

'Well, he knows who they are.'

She was a bit surprised. 'I know him. Does he have something to do with this?'

'No, miss. But the first time they picked on me he was there. He saw it, but he ran away.'

'OK. Just a moment, please,' she said, then left the room.

My mother and I began to whisper to each other

whilst she was out.

'Where do you think she's gone, Mum?'

'I don't know. All I know is she'd better get something done.'

'Let's just hope her best is good enough.'

Soon Mrs Martel was back.

'Right. We'll get to the bottom of this whatever it takes.'

She talked a little about the school's no-bullying policy and then Warren Stanmore came in. I could see that he didn't want to be there.

'Good morning, Warren,' said Mrs Martel.

He was gloomy. 'Good morning, Mrs Martel.'

'Now, Warren. I understand that you witnessed an episode of bullying involving four pupils and Jackson Jones. Can you tell me what you saw?'

Warren stood as if it was he that was in trouble, hands joined behind his back and head bowed. The words struggled to leave his mouth.

'One day last term I was talking to Jackson Jones in the playground and Terry Stock came up and slapped him in the back of his head. He began to say some stuff to him but I went, I didn't want any trouble.'

'OK, so it was Terry Stock, and who was with him?'

'Priti Shah, that's his girlfriend, and Alex Morris and his girlfriend, Lola, Lola Muir.'

Mrs Martel wrote the names down and asked, 'Did you see anything else, anything at all?'

'No,' said Warren. 'When they came all I wanted to do was get away.'

'OK, Warren. Thank you very much. You've been very helpful. You can go now.'

Warren left, but in all the time he was in the room he'd hardly looked at me. I wasn't sure if he hated me for naming him or if it was just the way he acted in such situations, because he didn't seem to look at any of us. When he was gone my mother and Mrs Martel came to an arrangement. I was to take the day off school and report to Mrs Martel the next morning; she was going to speak to the group. I was so relieved, I didn't want to be at school that day anyway.

My mother was extra nice to me that day. She spent a lot of time making sure I was feeling well and asking me if there was anything I needed. That was cool, but I didn't need kindness. I was feeling much better until the next morning when I had to go back to school. I went on my own and managed to go straight to Mrs Martel's office without being spotted by anyone, friend or foe. She was sounding very positive.

'Well, Jackson, I've had a word with Terry Stock and his friends, and although they didn't have much to say for themselves I have had assurances from them that they will modify their behaviour and stop their outbursts.'

This teacher speak didn't exactly fill me with

confidence and I made my feelings known.

'Modify their behaviour? Stop their outbursts? Mrs Martel, you can't believe them, I bet they didn't use that kind of language themselves, and just because you ask them to modify their behaviour and stop their outbursts doesn't mean they will.'

'I told them that I'll only be giving them one chance. If they are reported to me again all four of them will be excluded. Not only will they be excluded but if any of them are violent they will be reported to the police for assault. So you see, I am taking this very seriously.'

I was beginning to believe her. It sounded as if she was taking a zero-tolerance approach, which was just what I needed. Then she spoilt it all.

'Jackson,' she said.

'Yes, miss.'

'Is it true that you've been seeing Lionel Ferrier's mother?'

'Who told you that? It was them, wasn't it?'

'Does that matter?'

'Yes it does. Who told you?'

She walked to the large window and spoke with her back to me, looking out of the window.

'I know you have an interest in this whole Lionel and Ramzi thing, and most of us thought that what you were doing was harmless, but going to visit Miss Ferrier is very dangerous, and I gather that you even had her to your house for dinner. I appreciate that this may be none of my business, you're doing this in your personal time, but you have to draw the line somewhere. What does your mother think of this?'

'She's cool,' I said. 'She even cooked the food.'

Mrs Martel turned to face me and for the first time I saw that she could be an angry head mistress.

'You may think it's OK, your mother may think it's OK, but it's not OK. Just take a moment to think how Mrs Joseph would feel if she knew that you were getting so close to her husband's killer.'

'She does know,' I said.

'She does?'

'Yes,' I said. I was getting excited. 'Of course she knows, she was there. I wouldn't have done it without asking her first.'

Mrs Mertel walked over to me, disbelief clearly showing on her face.

'You mean to tell me that Mrs Joseph and Miss Ferrier sat at the same table with you and your mother and ate food together?'

'Yes.'

She walked back to the window and began to speak to me as she looked out of it again.

'If you have any problems with Terry Stock and his friends let me know immediately. I will not tolerate any bullying in this school. You can go to your lesson now.'

I said, 'Goodbye.'

She said, 'Goodbye.' But she didn't even turn round.

CHAPTER 23

On the Home Front

After school I thought it was time for me to report in to Mrs Joseph. I called my mother to tell her I'd be a bit late and then I called Mrs Joseph to arrange a meeting at the sports centre but she insisted that this time I should go to her house. From the outside Mrs Joseph's house looked like our house – all houses look the same in our area – but inside it was like a library. From the moment the door was open all I could see was books. The hallway was full of shelves that were full of books, the front door couldn't fully open because of them, and so it was up the staircase.

'Hello, Jackson. Come in,' said Mrs Joseph.

'Wow. So many books. Have you read them all?

'No,' she replied. 'I like reading but I'm not this mad about books. These were Edgar's, he was crazy about books. He used to say that he never read all of them but he knew what they were all about, and he knew where to look if he needed to find something out. I didn't believe him though.'

'What, you thought he was lying?'

'Yes.'

'You mean they were just for show?'

'No,' she said, waving her arms about. 'I mean I think he read all of them.'

'Wow,' I said again as she led me into the front room.

The front room was so full of books the walls could barely be seen. The seats were like museum pieces, old looking, with cloth upholstery with flowered patterns on them, and an oak table in the centre of the room had a large vase full of flowers on it. As I sat down though I noticed something was wrong, some-thing was different. It was the arrangement of the chairs. One was pointing towards a bookshelf, the one I sat on was placed straight in front of another one, and one just looked out into the street. Mrs Joseph sat on the one in front of me and I couldn't resist asking.

'Why are your chairs in these positions?'

'Oh, that,' she replied. 'I'm so used to them it's just normal for me. It's not so much about why the seats are like this. There's something else, haven't you noticed?'

I looked around the room, then I got it.

'No television. You've got no television.'

'That's right. Most living rooms are arranged around the television, all the chairs face the box, but when you take away the box you have the freedom to arrange the room to suit yourself. It's really liberating.'

'So you don't have a telly?'

'There is one, it's under the stairs somewhere. It's only small, so if I want to watch a programme I drag it out. I'm not really interested in most of the things on television nowadays. I listen to radio, classical music or talk radio, and it doesn't really matter where I sit to listen to that. I just make sure I have a radio in every room.'

That impressed me, I stored it somewhere in my mind as I did with many of the things that I planned to consider once I had my own place, then I began to tell her about my encounters with Terry Stock and his crew, and my visits to Mrs Martel.

'You did the right thing,' she said. 'You must report bullying as soon as you can. But why did they just pick on you like that?'

'I don't know. Some kids are like that. They just want to show off in front of their friends, or they just want to humiliate others.'

'So what happened when you went back to school? Did they bother you again?'

'No,' I replied. 'I saw them and they saw me but they stayed far away from me.'

'There you go. Hopefully they've learnt their lesson. Do you want a drink?'

'No thanks, I'm OK. I want to ask you something.'

'Go ahead,' Mrs Joseph said.

'What do you think now that you've met Miss Ferrier?'

'I thought she was a rather nice woman who has had a very sad life.'

'And you felt absolutely no anger towards her?'

'Absolutely none. I wouldn't mind meeting up with her again.'

Mrs Joseph's response was impressive, I thought.

'So what did you think of my mum?'

'She's great, you suit each other.'

'Don't tell her that,' I said. 'She thinks that *we* suit each other, me and you. We had a joke about you adopting me, or me having two mothers or something like that.'

She smiled. 'I'm not anti-kids but if I wanted any I would have had them a long time ago, and as nice as you are I don't think I would pass the test to adopt you. I think you have to like the idea of being a parent, and neither I nor Edgar ever did.'

Just then my mobile phone rang. I went to turn it off but I could see by the display that it was my mother. I apologised and answered it.

'Hello, Mum.'

She sounded tearful. 'Jackson, come here as quickly as you can. Something's happened.'

A shudder went through my body. 'What's happened, Mum? What is it?'

'Just come.'

'Tell me, Mum, what is it?'

'Someone's thrown bricks through the front

155

window and there's paint all over the front garden. I've called the police.'

'I'm coming,' I said.

I told Mrs Joseph what my mother said. She called a taxi and she insisted on going with me. When we arrived there was a police car outside the house with a few onlookers. The main front window was smashed and there was paint all over the front door and in the front garden. We ran inside, where my mother was just finishing an interview with a policewoman.

'Mum, are you OK?'

'Yes, I'm OK. Come here.'

I went to her and she put her arms around me and hugged me.

'What happened?' said Mrs Joseph.

'I was in the kitchen when I heard something, I didn't know what it was, it wasn't very loud, so I came into the front room, but I couldn't see anything. I was just walking over to the window to have a look outside and a brick came right through and just missed me. I couldn't believe it. I screamed and got down and lay on the floor but nothing else happened. Then one of the neighbours knocked on the door to see if I was all right. There's the brick there.' She pointed to a brick that was still on the carpet. The policewoman bent down and picked it up.

'I'll take this, she said.' She handed a piece of paper to my mother. 'Your crime report number is on there.

You'll need that for your insurance company, and my phone number's underneath it if you need me. Are you sure you have no idea who may have done it?'

'No,' said my mother.

'Let me know if you come up with any ideas.'

I had an idea who it was but I stayed silent.

'I'll see myself out,' said the officer.

'This is disgusting,' said Mrs Joseph to my mother. 'So what was the first noise you heard?'

'I didn't realise it at the time but it was the paint hitting the front door and landing in the front garden.'

'Disgusting,' said Mrs Joseph again.

Mrs Joseph stayed for a while. She made my mother sit down whilst she made her tea followed by a few glasses of something alcoholic, which I thought was very good of her. I didn't know how to act under these circumstances, so it took some of the pressure off me, and I think it helped my mother having another woman around. Mrs Joseph didn't leave until the double glazers had come and fitted a new window and the small group of people outside had gone. She offered to stay for the night but Mum thought she had done enough.

That night I slept very badly. I heard every time my mother turned in bed. I felt as if I was looking after a delicate child. I was also feeling guilty because I had pretty strong ideas about who had thrown that brick, but I kept my cool. I wanted to stay home the next day but my mother thought that I had already missed too many days off and ordered me to go to school. So I went, and the first thing I did when I got there was go to see Mrs Martel.

'Come in, Jackson,' she said from the other side of the door. She was sitting at her desk behind large stacks of papers. She pushed some of the papers aside to make room to rest her arms.

'I think I know why you're here. I told you that I wouldn't tolerate any bullying in this school and I meant it. Tell me what happened?'

'It's not just about bullying, miss, it's worse than that. Terry and his idiot friends attacked our house last night.'

I could see by the look on her face she hadn't heard about the attack.

'What do you mean, attacked your house?'

'They put a brick through our window and it just missed my mum.'

'Did you call the police?'

'Yes, my mum did.'

'So why weren't they arrested?'

'Because no one saw their faces. They were dressed in hoodies and they got away, but I know it was them.'

'Did you run after them?'

'I wasn't there. I got a call after it happened and I went straight home.'

I was beginning to know her well. I predicted what she would do next, and I was right. She stood up and walked over to the window.

'Did they do anything or say anything to you in or, for that matter, out of school?'

'No.'

'Well, then there's not much that I can do. They're no angels, we know that, but it may not have been them. If I don't have any evidence, then I can't do anything about it. You must know that, Jackson.'

'But they did it, miss.'

Mrs Martel continued to look out of the window. 'Get the evidence, give it to me or the police, and I promise you we'll nail them, but until then there's nothing I can do.'

I began to get that feeling again, my body temperature rising from the tips of my toes and the pit of my stomach, and I could feel tears coming again, but I wasn't going to cry in front of Mrs Martel.

'Can I go? I said.

'You came of your own free will, you can leave of your own free will, but be careful. Stay out of the way of Terry Stock and if you do come across them turn and go in another direction.'

I had no time for that teacher's speak.

'Can I go?'

'Of course you can.'

As I walked out, I was getting hotter. The school

secretary said goodbye but I ignored her. I walked into the playground. By this time I was burning up, and when I saw Terry Stock hanging with his friends I just jumped on his back and put my right arm around his neck.

'You smashed our window,' I shouted as I tried to strangle him and kick him at the same time, but all his friends just laughed. At this point I realised that I had forgotten something; I couldn't fight and I was probably the weakest boy in the school. Terry just walked in circles with me on his back as if I wasn't there.

'Has anyone seen that Jackson Jones by any chance?' he said sarcastically. 'He's around here somewhere.'

I used all the strength I had to try to strangle him but he just raised his shoulder, causing *me* pain, and continued to speak.

'Someone help me, I've got to find that Jackson Jones,' he said.

I flapped around on his back like a fish out of water until he just shook me off and I fell to the ground like a rucksack.

I was no fighter but I was angry.

'I hate you. You came round our house last night and smashed our windows, didn't you, didn't you? I'm going to get you.'

His friends were dancing with laughter. He stood over me like a giant.

160

'You can't even fight me from behind when I'm not looking, how do you plan to get me?'

I wasn't very tough, and I wasn't very good at sounding tough.

'I'm going to learn some moves,' I said.

The laughter grew as more people gathered round.

'He's gonna learn some moves,' said his girlfriend.

'Good idea,' said Terry. 'There's some judo lessons happening in town, sign up.'

I don't know what came over me. I jumped up and threw what felt like hundreds of kicks and punches to his body but they just seemed to bounce off, and the laughter got even louder. I decided to go for his face but fearing that I would hurt myself if I punched him I slapped him. He was unmoved. He laughed, clenched his fist, and brought his arm right back behind his head. I saw the punch coming towards me, so I closed my eyes and prepared myself to be knocked out, but the punch didn't come. I opened my eyes to see Mrs Cartwright the history teacher holding his arm back.

'OK,' she said. 'That's enough of that. Who started it?'

'It was him,' said Terry.

'Was it?' asked Mrs Cartwright.

I saw no reason to deny it.

'Yes, ' I said.

'Are you going to apologise?' she asked.

'No,' I said.

'Right. Report to Mrs Martel,' said Mrs Cartwright.

I took the blame for starting the fight, so I was the only one to face Mrs Martel. She told me that she knew that I would get myself in trouble after I left her office and that I had to think before I acted. She said I was a thoughtful young man who used to be a model student but she thought I may be losing my way. I wasn't very happy with her view of things, after all I was the victim, but I listened to her, told her I was sorry, and then left and went to my lesson.

CHAPTER 24

A Screen Test

For the rest of that day I was the laughing stock of the school, but it didn't bother me too much. Seeing my mother upset affected me much more, and I was feeling this urgent need to do something about it. Terry Stock and his gang were free to mock me and I wanted some revenge. It was a macho thing; the problem was I wasn't very macho. But it was the last day of the school week so I had the weekend to think things over.

My plan was to not let my mother out of my sight that weekend; her plan was to behave as normally as possible to get me out of the house, but there wasn't much to go out for. I had come to a dead end on the case and I wasn't making new friends. Then my mother gave me a job; I was to strip both the old and the unwanted new paint off the front door and repaint it, but first I had to clean the paving in the front garden. I was happy to do this. I got a broom for the broken glass and some turpentine for the paving and set to work. Although there was still a light stain on the paving where the paint had been I did a pretty good job with some moral support from passing neighbours. Then I started to strip the paint off the door with some paint stripper. I reached the point where my mind was willing but my arms were not, so I stopped. The paint from the door was stripped off but repainting would have to wait.

Turpentine and paint stripper is strange stuff; even after I showered I still smelt of the stuff, like a newly painted hospital ward. It wasn't nice, but it was slightly better than smelling like a toilet. I decided to go for a walk in the hope that the breeze would remove the offending odour. I walked a route that took me past my school and was surprised to see lots of activity there. The gates were open and there were four large trucks in the playground. I walked towards the gate and into the playground.

'Can I help you?' asked a woman holding a clipboard.

'Yes,' I said. 'I go to this school. What's happening here?'

'We're from Alpha Beta Films, an independent film company that specialises in taking on tough subjects, and we're making a documentary about the teacher who was murdered here.'

I was shocked. 'You're making a documentary? Who said you can?'

'Oh, we have permission,' she said, smiling. 'It's what we call a docudrama, a documentary with some acting in it to illustrate various events.'

'You can't make a silly docudrama,' I said. 'You

don't know anything. You don't know anything about this school and you don't know anything about the people in it.'

The woman was still trying to hang on to her smile.

'You're taking it a bit personally.'

'Of course I am, because I know that you don't know anything. I know more about this case than you.'

'So what do you know?'

I saw Mrs Martel walking across the far end of the playground.

'I'm not telling you,' I said, heading off towards Mrs Martel. 'Mrs Martel,' I shouted. She was walking away from me. 'Mrs Martel.'

Then I heard someone shout from one of the school doorways, 'Cut. Cut. Can someone get that boy out of shot?'

'Mrs Martel, what's happening?'

'They're making a documentary, and I think you just walked right into their shot. I'm supposed to be wandering around the school grounds thinking about life and looking very serious.'

I felt more heat building up inside me.

'Miss, you didn't tell me about this.'

'You didn't ask me. I know you have an interest in what happened but it's really none of your business.'

The man shouted from the doorway again.

'Alice, get that boy out of shot, will you? And Mrs Martel, I'm sorry about this, but could you come back and do that walk again?'

'OK,' she shouted back, and Alice, the woman I first spoke to when I entered the playground, came and asked me if could stay out of shot.

'I'm going now,' I said, but before I left I let Mrs Martel know that I thought what she was doing was wrong, and she told me that I was getting above my station. I didn't know that I had a station.

As Alice walked with me to the gate she told me that she had worked out who I was.

'Who am I?' I asked.

'I can't remember your name, but you're one of the lads who was nearby when Mr Joseph was stabbed, and you also became friends with Mrs Joseph afterwards. I was told that you became a right little private investigator. Would you come on the programme and tell us some of your experiences?'

'No way.'

'It wouldn't take up much time.'

'Never,' I said as defiantly as I could.

'But it would be really interesting to know about your friendship with Mrs Joseph. People would want to hear what you have to say. What drives you, what you thought of Mr Joseph, what did you think of the two boys who were prosecuted, stuff like that. There's even been talk about his mother, some say she's a little strange.'

'She's not strange.'

'You know her?' she asked, surprised.

'Yes I know her.'

'That's amazing,' she said, making a note on her clipboard. 'And what does Mrs Joseph think about the fact that you know her?'

I shook my head. 'Not you as well. Why do people think it's so strange that I know both of them? Miss Ferrier can't be blamed for the actions of her son, and Mrs Joseph knows that. They're both intelligent people.'

'That's fascinating,' she said. 'If you got involved in our programme maybe they would both agree to come on. We could even have a round-table discussion.'

I laughed.

'A round-table discussion? They don't need you to get a round-table discussion together. They've already spent an evening together at my house, why would they want to do it on camera?'

As I finished speaking I realised that I may have said too much. She began to get even more excited.

'You've got to come on the programme. You're passionate, articulate, and you would add an extra dimension to a programme which essentially is a programme about the human psyche and the dark forces that can afflict a juvenile mind. We promise it won't take much time, we can do it at your convenience, and we can pay you.'

I said, 'No, and no means no.'

Then I walked away, back to my house to spend time with my mother.

CHAPTER 25

Women's Talk

I did want to spend time with my mother but she was busy calling friends and going through what had happened to the house. So I called a friend.

'Hello, Mrs Joseph. You'll never believe what I saw today. I saw a film crew in school, and guess what, they're making a film about Mr Joseph and everything that happened. Can you believe that?'

'I know,' she said.

'You know?'

'Yes. I didn't know they were at the school today but I know they're making the film.'

'Who told you?'

'They did. They approached me and asked me if I wanted to be in it.'

'They did? And what did you say?'

'I said no of course. They said they wanted to give me the opportunity to speak for my husband but I just said he didn't need speaking for. I'm sorry, I forgot to tell you. I suppose I didn't think it was that important.'

'It's OK,' I said. 'I'm just a bit surprised. I can't imagine why Mrs Martel said yes.'

'Who knows? I wouldn't worry about it; she can only really talk about the school. She can't say that much about Edgar, she didn't know him that well, and she can't talk about Ramzi or Lionel. I know that Miss Ferrier refused to speak to them.'

I got even more surprised.

'What, they asked Miss Ferrier too? How do you know?'

'They told me.'

'I don't believe it,' I said. 'Well, they asked me too and I said no. I think I need to do some more investigations. I'll speak to you soon. Bye.'

'Be careful, Jackson. Bye now.'

Deep down inside I was hurt. I don't know if it was my ego or what, but I didn't like the fact that these developments had been happening without me knowing about them. I thought I knew more than anyone else about the case, and I probably did, but I hadn't known that a film was being made about it, I had accidentally stumbled upon it.

I woke up tired after a night of very little sleep. It was early but it suited me just fine, it was a perfect time to go and see Miss Ferrier. I knew what Sunday mornings were like on Fentham Road. Peaceful. When I arrived at her house it looked very quiet. I was worried, if she was still asleep I didn't want to wake her. I pressed the bell lightly but it rang really loud, and then I listened for Miss Ferrier. I heard movement, then I heard that familiar call.

'Who is it?'

'It's OK, Miss Ferrier.' I said. 'It's only me, Jackson.'

'Wait a minute,' she said, and I waited.

I knew that the first thing I had to do was apologise for waking her up so early, so in my head I was running through possible wordings of my apology. She called me again, I looked up, and the world turned gold. Another warm shower, another bucket of urine in my face.

'Miss Ferrier,' I shouted through the mist. 'It's me, Jackson.'

'I know it's you, now go away before the weather turns again.'

'Miss Ferrier, what's wrong? I thought we were friends, what did I do?'

'You know what you did,' she shouted. 'You went and told the film company where I live. Just because I went to your house that doesn't mean we're going to start making films together, you know. I trusted you, I thought you were different; I even let you come in my house. Who told you to go giving my address to the television people? I don't want to be on any freak show.'

I shook my head to get rid of as much of the bodily fluid as I could and began pleading with her.

'Honest, Miss Ferrier, I didn't tell them anything. I only found out about the film yesterday. I was just walking past school and I saw them filming.'

'Go away,' she said. 'And don't come back round here. I thought you were different, I thought that I could trust you. You are just like the rest, I should have known it.'

I could see I wasn't going to win the argument, so I took my jacket off, slung it over my shoulder and walked home.

I managed to get into my room and change my clothes and then I locked myself in my bedroom and washed them. I was desperate to hide my misfortune from my mother, so I hung the wet clothes in my wardrobe to dry. I couldn't tell my mother about what had happened but the next thing I did was call Mrs Joseph and tell her everything. She was sympathetic, but the mention of urine still brought a giggle. Things didn't get easier. As we were ending the call she asked if I could do her a favour.

'Jackson, could you give me her address?'

I was astonished that she'd asked me.

'I just told you that she was blaming me for giving the TV people her address and now you want me to give her address to you. She'd kill me.'

'I see your point, but I think there's a big difference

171

between the TV people and me.'

'I'm not sure if she'll care about that. She just hates me again, and I don't want to stir things up again.'

'Listen, Jackson,' she said, sounding like my mother. 'Can you trust me?'

'Yes.'

'Well, trust me, then.'

'I'm confused,' I admitted.

'Trust me, I really need to speak to her – if there's a problem I'll take the blame. It will be OK.'

I thought about it very hard. Then I said, 'No.'

'Come on. Look, I know she lives on Fentham Road, she told me, so all you have to do is tell me the number. If I just took a walk I could probably find out anyway.'

I thought about it very hard. She was right, she could find it anyway, and I was sure that Miss Ferrier would still see her as a friend, unlike a television company. Then I said, 'Number thirty-five.'

She said, 'Thanks, Jackson.'

I said, 'She'll probably never speak to me again.'

I could almost hear her already putting on her coat when I told her the number, so I was worried, very worried. And I was even more worried when I didn't hear from her for the rest of the day.

Once again I woke up tired after another night of very little sleep, but this time I had to go to school. How things change. I actually used to love going to school, and I was one of the few people I knew who loved Monday mornings, but not any more. I had the Terry Stock lot on my mind, and I wasn't in the mood to exchange smiles with the head teacher. As I entered the school I saw Priti Shah and Lola Muir, the girls of the gang.

'Hello, Jackson,' said Priti.

'Don't come anywhere near me,' I replied, trying to sound threatening.

They just giggled to each other.

'Don't worry,' said Lola. 'We're not going anywhere near you. Why would we want to do that, why would anyone want to do that?'

'Just leave me alone. That's all.'

'Or you'll tell your friend Mrs Martel and we'll get something really horrible like detention.'

'I have nothing more to say,' I said and I walked away.

It was just starting to rain, so I went into the school building to stay dry. That's what I told myself I was doing as I headed in, but the truth was I didn't like the idea of being in the playground. As well as my new enemies I had become a bit of a joke to many of the other kids. I was the nerdy kid who fancied himself as a cop and couldn't fight his way out of his shirt. As I was walking down the main corridor I saw Mrs Martel coming towards me. I really didn't want to have to speak to her either but it was too late to change direction or nip into a classroom.

She stopped directly in front of me with the grace of a soldier on parade.

'Good morning, Jackson,' she said as if she was addressing a multitude of people.

'Good morning,' I mumbled.

'Are you unwell?' she asked.

'No, miss.'

'Is there something wrong?

'You know what's wrong, miss. You know I think you shouldn't be agreeing to be in that film.'

'Now, Jackson. I think you're a nice boy but I can't look for your approval for everything I do in this school, and there is nothing in the film, as far as I know, that offends other people.'

I felt it was important for her to know the strength of my feeling.

'I think you're wrong, miss.'

'And I think you're wrong, Jackson.'

'But, miss –'

'Look, Jackson,' she interrupted. 'Just leave it, will you? What's done is done; soon it will be on television and then you'll see that it's just a bit of entertainment.'

'Entertainment, a bit of entertainment, and you think that's OK?'

'Forget it.'

'I won't forget it, miss.'

'If you can't forget it, get over it. Good morning, Jackson,' she said, walking away.

The good thing about not having lots of friends at school was not having lots of distractions. On the other hand being on your own in a corner of a playground that was full of kids playing with each other was a very lonely place to be. But it was a good time to think. Not having to fit in with any group in the classroom meant that I was able to focus on my work. It wasn't fun but I was very productive that day. As I was leaving the school I saw a couple of vans belonging to the film company. On the far side of the road cameras were set up and Alice was loitering on the pavement. My plan was to say nothing but as I walked past them Alice recognised me.

'Hi, remember me?'

'No,' I said. 'I don't know you.'

'You remember me, I saw you here yesterday.'

'Oh yes. I remember now. What are you doing today?'

'We're just getting some shots of kids leaving the school.'

'Please make sure I'm not in any of those shots. You didn't tell me that you spoke to Mrs Joseph.'

'You didn't ask me,' she replied. 'I spoke to her today too.' She passed me her business card. It was embossed and had a small photo of her on it. 'If you ever change your mind give me a call.'

After all I had said to her the day before I felt this was a bit of an insult, but I didn't want to lose my cool, not with all the kids passing. But I wanted to give her a piece of my mind. I put the card in my pocket, and said, 'If you ever change your mind – give your conscience a call.'

I arrived home to be greeted by the bare wood of our front door. I made a mental note to finish the job.

I went into the house, hung up my coat in the hallway and walked into the front room. What I saw not only surprised me, it also frightened me. My mother, with Mrs Joseph and Miss Ferrier, all sitting together. I did a reality check.

'Mum, Miss Ferrier, Mrs Joseph. What are you all doing here?'

'Well, I live here,' said my mother.

'And I've just popped in to see how your mother was,' said Mrs Joseph.

'And I've come to apologise,' said Miss Ferrier.

'Apologise for what?'

'For my latest downpour, and for not believing you. Mary has explained everything to me and I'm sorry for thinking you gave the film people my address. They did all that research stuff they do, they probably got it from the voters' list at the town hall.'

'And I found your clothes in the wardrobe,' said my

mother. 'I've given them another wash and put them on the line. The fresh air will do them good.'

'Oh, Mum,' I said, unable to hide my embarrassment. I turned to Mrs Joseph and Miss Ferrier. 'It's OK. I'm just glad that you both turned down the film.'

Mrs Joseph stood up.

'We're not doing the film, but tomorrow morning we are doing breakfast television.'

I couldn't believe what I was hearing.

'You're doing what?'

'Breakfast television,' she continued. 'The film company are making a film that's more about drama than the truth, and there are so many rumours going around. Some people think Miss Ferrier's a witch, some people think we hate each other, some think that I am mad for not wanting revenge. I had a phone call from my lawyer who said I had been invited on after the press found out about the film being made. We've talked about it, and we think that the best thing we can do is show unity and put the record straight, once and for all.'

I was flabbergasted, but unlike the so-called docudrama I could see the sense in this and I told them so. I then begged Miss Ferrier never to shower me with gold again and she promised she wouldn't. I then begged all three of them to allow me to go with them to the television station the next morning, only to be greeted with three speeches on how important it was for me to go to school. I tried to convince them that it was a special occasion, that a morning off wouldn't herald the end of my education, but they were united in their dismissal of my excuses. The only good thing was that they were on air early enough for me to watch them before I went to school.

Considering that it was me that originally brought them together I felt very left out that night. I warmed up some leftovers from the fridge and went to my room, leaving them to talk about stuff I supposedly didn't understand. I had some homework to do but I opted to spend most of the night looking through a decorating catalogue, trying to decide on a new colour for the front door. It was hard being the man of the house.

CHAPTER 26

Together

I had set the alarm on my mobile phone to ring early in the morning. I heard it, but I heard it somewhere in the distance, like background noise in my dream. After a prolonged snooze I jumped up and called my mother but there was no response, so I got up and went to her bedroom and knocked on the door, but there was still no response. There was also no response when I shouted downstairs, at which point I realised that she had already left. I turned the television on and a woman who looked too happy for her own good was making an announcement.

'Our next item concerns the tragic story of the teacher who was fatally stabbed in his own playground. The story hit the headlines earlier this year and two young boys are serving long sentences for the murder. But who would have thought that the mother of one of the killers and the wife of the murdered teacher would become friends? They'll both be joining me, after the news and weather.'

I ran around the house readying myself for school

and then I headed for the kitchen. I had two choices. I could attempt to cook myself something quite substantial, which I thought I deserved, or I could just grab myself something quick and easy. I went for the quick option, the super-quick option. I simply grabbed a box of cereal and took it to the living room, where I just thrust my hand into the box and scooped up mouthfuls of crispy stuff. It was almost time to leave for school when the weather was over and the happy lady was back on screen.

'And now. If your husband, or one of your relatives, was murdered by a boy, could you become friends with the boy's mother? That's exactly what happened after the murder of Edgar Joseph, the school teacher who was killed by a pupil at Marston Hall school. Mary Joseph was seen as a caring wife in mourning, Lisa Ferrier was seen as a neglectful mother who didn't care about the upbringing of her son. In a remarkable twist in this real-life drama they have struck up a friendship, something which some people find rather hard to understand given the circumstances. They both join me on the sofa now. Let me start with you, Mary. After the loss of your husband you must have done a lot of grieving. The whole country sympathised with you and his killers became figures of hatred. What made you want to befriend the mother of one of his killers?'

Mrs Joseph looked very relaxed, almost as if she

had just come out the swimming pool.

'Well, it wasn't my idea; it was the idea of a young friend that Lisa and I have in common. When he put the idea to me that we should meet I hesitated at first, but then I thought about it and I thought, why not? She hadn't done anything to me. So it made sense. I had already realised that Lisa was not the monster they were painting in the media and I have always tried to look behind the headlines, even when the headlines concern me.'

'But it has been difficult for you,' said the presenter. 'Didn't you feel anger towards Lisa? What do you talk about when you're together?'

Mrs Joseph smiled. 'No, I don't feel any anger towards Lisa, and, shock horror, when we get together we talk about the things other women talk about. This morning for example we were talking about you.'

'Is that all?'

'And we were taking about coming on the show, and what to wear. We are both ordinary women. We can't all be TV presenters.'

The presenter wasn't amused. 'Don't you ever talk about the death of your husband?'

'Maybe once,' said Mrs Joseph, 'when we first met, but we have a lot more in common than the tragedy that visited us.'

The presenter picked up a newspaper that was on

the table in front of her.

'A couple of days ago a national newspaper accused you of joining the killers' side. They said you are a traitor to the cause of the victims of crimes.'

'There are no sides here,' said Mrs Joseph. 'There are no winners and no losers, but there are many victims, and this is not a game.'

'Can I come to you now, Lisa?' said the presenter, pivoting on her seat. 'I don't want to repeat all the things that have been said about you in the press, but it could be said that going public with your friendship is a way of hiding behind the goodwill of Mary and cleaning up your image.'

Miss Ferrier's demeanour was the opposite of Mrs Joseph's. She was nervous, hesitant, leaving long pauses in between words.

'I – I don't think I'm hiding behind anything – I never thought of – being like – friendly with Mary – but we just did. It was really because of one boy – he's a pupil at the school – I thought he was a bit mad myself but he knew I wasn't mad or – or cruel – or a witch. He's a good lad.'

'Can I just say something?' said Mrs Joseph. 'I am sick and tired of the way people are blaming Lisa for what her son did. He did a bad thing, I know that more than anyone else in the world, but he did it, not Lisa. The reason we are here today is because there is a documentary about this whole affair being made right now and it may make good TV but it's not telling the whole truth. For example, I'm told that there's a dramatic reconstruction of me phoning Lisa and shouting at her down the phone. I never did that.'

'I haven't even got a phone,' said Miss Ferrier.

Mrs Joseph continued, 'And apparently Lisa was supposed to have lied to the police when they came to her house looking for Lionel. It's just not true. Lionel didn't even make it home; he was arrested in the park not long after the stabbing. We want to show people that we are not bitter with each other. Lisa hates what her son did as much as I do and whatever the film says we know the truth and we have come to tell the truth.'

'That's very brave,' said the presenter.

'I don't think it's brave. I can't hate her, there's too much hate in the world. We have to move on.'

Miss Ferrier butted in nervously, 'I think she's brave. She could have just turned against me like so many people have – but she has done the opposite, she has really helped me realise that I have nothing to be ashamed of.'

'Well,' said the presenter, returning to her happy face, 'this is quite a story. What do you think people can learn from your experiences?'

Miss Ferrier spoke first.

'I was beginning to think everyone hated me because of something I never done, but now I've learnt that there are good people out there.'

Mrs Joseph then said, 'I just want to thank Jackson Jones and his mother for bringing us together – I don't like being in the public, and I don't want to be hounded by the press or programme-makers and I don't want to do breakfast TV chat shows any more. All I have to say is leave us alone and I'd also like to say we all must save a space in our hearts for forgiveness.'

The presenter turned to the camera.

'An amazing pair. We've come to the end of this morning's show. It only remains for me to thank you for joining us. We'll be back tomorrow morning at six a.m. See you then. Goodbye.'

I looked down and my lap was covered with cereal, I looked up and the clock was saying eight forty-five. I ran to clean my teeth, shouting, 'Oh no, I'm late.'

CHAPTER 27

The Lady in Question

Mrs Martel was waiting for me as I entered the school.

'I'm glad you could make it, Jackson.'

'I'm sorry I'm late, miss, it won't happen again,' I said, rushing past her.

'One minute, Jackson.'

I stopped.

'Can I see you in my office?'

'When?'

'Now.'

'But I've go to go to registration, miss.'

'Don't worry,' she said. 'I've dealt with that.'

She led the way and I walked behind her feeling naughty but nice. When we reached her office she walked over to the window, looked out, and started by congratulating me.

'Well done, Jackson. I saw the programme this morning and I have to say I was very impressed. You did a great thing by bringing them together and it was quite a feat getting them on television.'

'I got them together, but it was their idea to go on TV.'

'Yes, but it wouldn't have happened without you. I've done my bit in the documentary now but I want you to know that I haven't got involved in this character assassination that's been going on. All I did was let them film around the school and I did a short interview saying that we were a pretty normal school, and Mr Joseph was a pretty good teacher.'

'What did you say about Lionel?' I asked.

'Nothing,' she replied. 'I just said I didn't know him very well, but I've read his reports and he seemed like an average pupil. Anyway, they've done all they need to do here; they'll be finishing the film elsewhere now, so you can stop being angry with me. Are you still angry with me?'

'You told me *what* you did, but I still don't understand *why* you did it,' I replied.

Mrs Martel turned to face me and looked at me for a couple of seconds. Without taking her eyes off me she took a couple of steps forward and stood next to her desk. Then came the confession.

'I really did think it was harmless, and we – that's me and you, and everybody else in this school – really need the money. They offered us a lot of money for a couple of days' filming. You may think that all I do is watch teachers and parade through the corridors but there's more to being a head teacher than that.

Nowadays I have a budget to manage, books to balance, I have to spend money, save money, and make money. It's called the internal market. I didn't do it because I wanted to see myself on television, no, that money has gone straight into the school funds to help pay for some of the things this school desperately needs.'

'I understand,' I said.

She smiled; it was the first time she'd smiled in my presence for a long while.

'I could talk about the changing role of a head teacher for a long time. Another time, maybe. Now to your class – don't worry, I warned Mrs Anderson that you'd be late.'

Word had got around the school that I had been mentioned on breakfast television that morning, but there was very little mention of the context. Most people thought I was just stirring trouble. I had a lot of thinking to do, so I made sure I stayed out of people's way. I used my loneliness to think about the journey I'd been on and what I had discovered about Mrs Joseph, Miss Ferrier, Lionel and Ramzi. There was a lot to think about but one thing was for sure, my view of all of them had changed, and I still thought there was more to learn.

When I arrived home that afternoon the three women in my life were in the living room talking about the programme. Although my mother had only watched it from the side of the studio she was apparently the most nervous. At one point I even heard them talking about forming a support group of some kind, and then a writers' group, and then a chess group. I realised that they weren't serious when they started talking about a Jackson Jones support group. It was good to see them happy, most of all Miss Ferrier.

That evening we ate together. This time all three of them helped with the cooking and I pretended to do my homework. I have no idea what time Miss Ferrier and Mrs Joseph left, but I do remember falling asleep to the sound of them mimicking the voice of the TV presenter with the happy face. I'm pretty sure they were up until the early hours of the morning, but they were happy, so I was happy.

I had pleasant dreams, and happiness was still with me at the breakfast table, where my mother had to listen to me telling bad jokes about the TV presenter. My ability to tell jokes was as bad as my ability to defend myself but she was happy to go along with me. Just when I thought she was sounding more like the sister I never had than my mother, she jumped up off her chair and said, 'Right, now off to school, young man. And remember, you owe me some good exam results.'

I went through my packing routine and made my

way to school. I was happy, until I reached the school gate, where Terry Stock, Priti Shah, Alex Morris and Lola Muir were standing. They stood on the playground side of the gate, Terry and Priti on one side of the gate and Lola and Alex on the other. I stopped. If I was going to go in I would have to walk between them. There was an alternative. As I thought about it Alex Morris seemed read my mind.

'Come on, Detective Inspector Jackson. Enter, or if you don't like the look of this entrance there's always the other one.'

The other one was a bit of a walk away and I didn't fancy the walk there, and more importantly I didn't want them to think I was intimidated. It's hard not to look intimidated when you are.

'You don't frighten me, you know,' I said, frightened.

'You frighten me,' said Terry. 'No, you don't frighten me, I just feel sorry for you. It must be so hard being a freak.'

I tried a threat. 'If you touch me –'

'You'll tell Mrs Martel,' said Lola interrupting.

Not wanting to feel left out Priti said her bit.

'Come on, wacky jacky, we're not going to touch you.'

I decided to walk through. Step one was good, step two was good, but on the third step Terry shouted, 'Boo.'

I jumped as if a firework had gone off under my

feet, and then I ran as if I had ants in my pants. They laughed as if it was very funny. I wanted to report them but I just couldn't see myself running to Mrs Martel saying. 'Miss, they said boo to me and laughed at me.'

I let it go and just avoided them throughout the day, but I was to see them again when school was over. As I headed towards the street I heard a commotion. The noise was loud and there was a large group of kids gathered around the gate area. I ran over and saw about ten kids shouting abuse at the woman who had been in court claiming to be Ramzi's mother. She looked rough, as if she hadn't slept, washed or eaten for days. A couple of people started throwing paper balls and chewing gum at her.

'My boy's better than all of you,' she shouted back at them.

'Your boy's in the nick,' shouted Terry. 'And he's not your boy anyway. You're too old for him and he doesn't date women with hairy chests.'

'You're a smelly tramp, Mrs, you know that, don't you?' shouted Lola.

'And your hair's like animal farm,' said another girl, trying to get noticed.

The insults began to come from all directions before someone shouted, 'Teacher. Run.'

And they ran, leaving about five boys including myself standing there as the teacher joined us. One of the boys was Warren Stanmore; the teacher was a supply teacher who had just finished her first day at the school.

'What's going on here?' she said, looking from us to the woman.

'I don't know,' I said.

The others claimed ignorance too, but I knew they knew more than me. One of them must have seen how it all started.

The teacher shouted to the woman on the other side of the railings, 'Are you all right there?'

'No I'm not all right,' she shouted back. 'I hate this school, I hate those kids, and I want to kill all of you because you lot killed my son.'

The teacher had no idea what she was going on about. She turned to us again.

'What does she mean by you lot killed my son?'

'Don't worry, miss, she's the local mad woman, she's always letting off,' said one of the boys as he picked up his bag and walked off.

'She's not mad,' said Warren. 'She just needs help.' He began to walk off, following the other boy, but as he did so I heard him mutter, 'And she needs a son.'

'OK,' said the teacher. 'Let's go.'

The two boys who were left walked off in one direction and I chased after Warren. He walked swiftly down the road. As I spoke to him he looked straight ahead.

'Warren, what do you mean when you say she needs a son?'

'I ain't telling you anything.'

'What's the matter?'

'You talk too much, and you ask too much questions. Then when I tell you stuff you grass me up.'

'I don't grass you up, I'm just trying to work all this stuff out.'

'Well, I'm not telling you anything,' he said, trying to quicken his pace.

'So what do you know?'

'I know more than you, but why should I tell you anything?'

'Because I need to know,' I shouted, surprising myself by my own strength of feeling. 'I know there's more to all this, but what is it?'

'Just leave me alone, man. Go and ask the old lady, leave me alone.'

I jumped in front of him so that he couldn't walk any further. He tried to sidestep me but I moved with him.

'Do you know that lady?' I asked.

'Kind of.'

'Kind of what?'

'I kind of know her,' he said.

'Is she Ramzi's mum?'

'Kind of.'

'What do you mean, kind of? Is she or isn't she?'

'Kind of.'

I got loud again. 'Kind of what? Answer the question, will you?'

Warren raised his head and looked at me. 'I'm not saying any more, just go and ask her. Now let me go, or I'll report *you* for bullying.'

'OK. Thanks anyway, Warren. Thanks. I'll go and ask her.'

'Good.'

I walked away slowly, and then I began to hurry. Then Warren shouted, 'Jackson.' He had his hands around his mouth, directing his voice in my direction. 'Ask her about the cider,' he shouted.

'The what?' I shouted back, unsure of what he said.

'The cider,' he shouted again.

I sprinted back to the school as quickly as I could but when I arrived she had gone. I ran up and down the side streets but I couldn't see her anywhere. There were still stragglers on the streets from school, so I began to ask them. No one had seen her, and then I got lucky. A girl told me that she had just seen her heading back towards the school. She told me which route she had taken and I sprinted off. I arrived back at the school just in time to see her taking stones from a hat that she had in her hands and throwing them into the playground. They went nowhere near the school building, but I felt I had to stop her. I ran to her.

'Excuse me. You don't know me, but –'

'Don't talk to me,' she said.

'I don't want to talk to you,' I said. 'I want to talk with you.'

'What's the difference?' she said, throwing the minute stones in the playground.

'The difference is that I listen to you.'

She stopped throwing. 'What do you want?'

'Is Ramzi your son?'

'Yes,' she said.

'Did he ever live with you?'

'Sometimes. Well, he didn't really live with me but he spent a lot of time with me.'

I was confused but I felt she was opening up, so I trod carefully.

'Trust me when I say that I really don't want to sound rude, but did you give birth to him.'

She was quick to answer. 'No, but he is my son. Giving birth is only a small part of being a mother. I didn't give birth to him but it was me that took care of him, it was me that he came to when he had problems, and it was me that gave him the love that he needed. I don't care what anyone else says, that makes him my son.'

Her tone was very aggressive. I now realised that the idea of Ramzi being her son was a fantasy in her head but I tried to talk to her more to calm her down without questioning her logic.

'Was he a good son?'

'Yes, he was a good son. The people he lived with just gave him a house, but I gave him a home. He didn't live with me but I gave him a home.' She suddenly sat down on the wall where the railings went into the concrete, and I joined her. 'I saw you in court, didn't I?' she asked.

'Yes.'

'You think I'm a mental case too, don't you?'

'No.'

'I had a husband once, you know, and a son. They both died in a fire. It was my fault, they were sleeping upstairs in the nice house we used to have, and I was downstairs. I woke up, didn't I, needed a smoke. Sat on the settee, started smoking a fag and fell asleep. When I woke up everything was on fire. I tried to run upstairs but I couldn't. Some neighbours broke down the front door and got me out but it was too late for them. They sent me to the mental home, but I'm not mental, I just couldn't take the stress. That was in another area, a nicer area, in a nice part of town. We had money then, we were doing well, but I lost the house. No insurance, lost my husband, lost my son. You wouldn't understand.'

'It's hard for me to understand,' I said. 'But I'm trying to.'

Her voice got aggressive again.

'It's my fault, and you know what? I heard them

screaming. Can you imagine what it's like to hear your family screaming and you can't do anything?'

'No, I can't,' I said. It was all I could say.

She dropped her voice again. 'Care in the community. That's what they gave me, but no one cared. Then I met Ramzi. The social services people got me a room and Ramzi lived down the road from me. He looked after me and I looked after him. He used to drop in and see me, he said he would be my son, so he was.'

Slowly it was beginning to make sense, but there was something that was bugging me.

'He really was your son. Can you tell me about the cider?'

Once again she raised her voice and became aggressive.

'What do you want to know about the cider, who told you anything about the cider?'

'Please,' I pleaded. 'I don't mean any harm, I don't hate Ramzi – your son, I just need to know about the cider.'

She was silent for a while, and then she said. 'He just liked cider.'

'Did he used to get drunk?'

'I don't know. I never saw him drink a drop, I would have to buy it for him, then he and his friend would take it away. A lot of cider, a lot of the time.'

'And you never saw him drink any?'

'I just told you, no.'

I stood up. 'I'm really sorry about what happened to you, but thanks for talking to me. Honest, I'm not like the rest.'

'I know,' she said. 'You're nice. Do you want to be my son?'

I felt awkward. I really didn't want to offend or upset her.

'I have three mums already. Join the queue.'

For the first time I saw a tiny little smile on her face.

'I have to go now,' I said. 'Which way are you going? Let's walk together.'

'No. I want to stay here for a while. I'll be all right. You go on.'

'Take care,' I said and I left.

What she told me had numbed me. I felt as if I walked the first part of my journey home without looking where I was going. There was so much to think about. Things were coming together now but I really couldn't understand what Warren meant when he mentioned the cider. It felt like such an odd thing to throw in the mix. I had to find out more, so I ran to Bevington Road where Warren lived. When I got there Warren was riding his bicycle up and down the street with a friend. I shouted to him.

'Warren. Please, man, I need to talk to you.'

'You again,' he said as he skidded around me,

followed by his friend.

'Who's this?' asked his friend.

'He's just a friend from school,' said Warren. 'Well, sometimes he's a friend.'

I walked away. 'Come here, Warren. I need to speak to you in private.'

Warren followed me and his friend rode off.

'Warren, you got to tell me. What's this about the cider?'

'Didn't she tell you?'

'I asked her and she said she used to give Ramzi lots of cider.'

'There you are, then.'

'But what does that mean? She said she never saw him drink any.'

'That's because he didn't drink.'

'I've got it,' I said. 'He gave the drink to Lionel.'

'No. Lionel didn't drink either.'

Frustrated, I stamped my foot on the ground. 'I don't get it.'

'Walk down the road,' said Warren.

I began to walk and he pushed his bike and walked with me. After a short silence he began to speak.

'Lionel and Ramzi were weird, but they weren't tough. Have you ever seen them fight?'

'No,' I replied.

'Once they were beaten up by Terry Stock and his gang, and after that they bullied them all the time.

198

First of all they made them do weird things, then they made them bring them sweets and stuff, and then they made them bring cider in for them. Ramzi got the cider from the old lady, as long as he visited her she gave him anything he wanted. So he asked for lots of cider because he couldn't buy it in the shops. She needed someone that she could treat like a son, he needed to supply the bullies with cider. They were under pressure, man. That's all I know. Every day they would have to get cider. They were weirdoes but I felt sorry for them. Right, that's it. I gotta go.'

We stopped walking. 'Thanks, man,' I said.

'Don't tell anybody I told you stuff.'

'I promise, I won't. Trust me.'

He rode off to join his friend, and I went home to eat and sleep on it all.

CHAPTER 28

They All Fall Down

New questions were being thrown up all the time. I didn't know the old lady's name but the conversations I had had with her and Warren were being replayed in my mind again and again. I really didn't want to go to school the next day but I couldn't think of an excuse to tell my mother. There was also the small matter of the law of the land that I was becoming so keen on upholding, so I went. With all that on my mind I couldn't control my need to keep asking questions, but I knew I had to be careful.

I picked out a few kids and discreetly asked them if they were ever friends with Ramzi or Lionel, but it was as I thought, they didn't make a habit of making friends. I got another lead though when I spoke to a girl in our class, Anna Zelensky. When I asked her if she knew much about Ramzi or Lionel, she said, 'No, don't be stupid. Everyone knows they were loners. I shouldn't say this but I used to really feel sorry for them. I know they killed Mr Joseph but I really felt sorry for them.'

'Why?'

'Because people picked on them so much. Even on the day they killed Mr Joseph they were being bullied, but because everyone was concentrating on Mr Joseph no one asked about that. Nobody said anything about the bullying because that would make you look like you were sticking up for them. Nobody asked about them because they were seen as the baddies.'

'I am,' I said. 'I'm asking about them.'

'Only now, when it's too late, and even now what do you know? Do you know about Lionel's dad?'

'Yes.'

'Do you know about the animals?'

'Yes.'

'Did you know that Terry Stock and his horrible friends used to force them to bring them stuff. Pens, money, watches?'

'Cider,' I interrupted.

'Yes, cider,' she said. 'It's a real shame. Even the day before the killing I saw Ramzi and Lionel on their knees while Terry and them were pushing them and telling them to bring cider the next day.'

'What, you saw that, did you?'

'I saw it all right, right in front of me. I've even seen Lola, Priti, Terry and Alex drinking the cider after school and laughing their heads off.'

'Were you there when Mr Joseph was stabbed?'

'No. I came after it was all over.'

I thanked her and moved on but just as I was walking into the building another girl in our class, Martina Telford, approached me.

'Hey, Jackson, have you and Terry Stock been fighting?'

'No.'

'Oh, I was told that you and his lot were at war.'

'Well, they tried to push me around a bit, and someone threw paint over my house and smashed my window, and I think it was them. That's it really. I don't know if that's called war, I ain't doing any fighting.'

'I can't stand that lot. Did Terry pull his knife on you?' she asked.

'No,' I replied, surprised. 'Has he got one?'

'I saw him with one. He was showing off with it to his friends. Sharpening it and doing his stabbing movements.'

'Why don't you tell a teacher?'

'Because I haven't seen him with one lately. I'm talking about ages ago, I think it was in April or something. Yeah, April, the same day that Mr Joseph was killed.'

My thinking quickened. 'The day Mr Joseph was killed?'

'Yeah, but when I saw them they were outside of school. Around the side of the newsagent's on Gower Street. '

'Did they see you?'

'Yeah, and they chased me and told me to mind my own business, that's why I don't go anywhere near them.'

'Why didn't you tell the police? You know that Mr Joseph was killed by a knife,' I asked.

'They didn't kill Mr Joseph, and anyway I was scared, and I don't mind saying it. I didn't want them to start picking on me.' Suddenly she turned and ran into the school. 'Later.'

Her place was taken by Terry Stock and Alex Morris. They pushed me into a corner and moved in on me so that it was hard for anyone to see me.

'Leave me alone,' I said. 'You know what Mrs Martel said, you have to leave me alone.'

'Are you looking for trouble?' said Terry.

'Just leave me alone.'

'Just shut up. We'll leave you alone if you leave her alone.'

'Leave who alone?' I asked.

'Her, that girl you were just talking to,' said Alex.

'What's so important about her?' I said.

'Just leave her alone.'

In an attempt to sound tough I said, 'Say if I don't?'

Terry turned his back to me and thrust his elbow into my stomach, reminding me that I wasn't tough.

'That's what,' he said.

'What's she to you anyway?' asked Alex.

Terry turned back round and they both pushed themselves into me so hard that I felt embedded into the wall.

Terry spoke in one ear. 'Just ease off.'

And Alex spoke in the other. 'Or you're dead.'

They then walked off briskly and so did I, straight to the school secretary, where I demanded to see Mrs Martel. Maybe it was because of the speed that I spoke at and my roughed-up look, but the secretary looked scared. She made her call and showed me into the head teacher's office. I didn't wait for Mrs Martel to speak; I was shivering with anger as I spoke.

'Mrs Martel, Terry Stock just elbowed me. Him and Alex Morris threatened me.'

'When was this?'

'Just now, miss, as I was walking into the school. You got to do something about it, miss, you said you would.'

'I did, and I will. You can rest assured that I will punish them severely. OK, go and get registered and I'll speak to you later today after I have decided what steps to take.'

'I'm not just going back out there as if nothing's happened, you have to do something about it now.'

She went back to her window. 'I can't do anything right now, these things take time.'

'They'll just deny it or something, call them now, miss, let them face me now.'

'I can't,' she said.

'You can,' I insisted.

She turned to me. 'You can't tell me what I can and can't do.'

'They've been identified, they have been given a warning, what else do you want?'

'I need to hear their side of the story.'

'I want them to face me now, here.'

'Why, what difference will it make? I can't understand why you don't just let me do things my way.'

Then I told her what was really on my mind. 'Because I think they should face their victim, and I think they should face the truth.'

I wasn't sure how to connect my next sentence, so I left a pause before speaking as slowly and as clearly as I could.

'I think they had something to do with the killing of Mr Joseph, miss.'

She laughed, as all adults seem to do when they don't believe something.

'Don't talk rubbish. As you know there's been a full police inquiry, and a court trial for that matter, and the case is closed.'

'The police asked a lot of questions, but there were a lot of questions they didn't ask. And the trial, you were there, because they pleaded guilty there was no trial.'

'This is ridiculous,' said Mrs Martel. 'I'm not going

down this path. The case is closed and that's that. It's over.'

I could see that I had to use a more relevant reason to get them in Mrs Martel's office.

'OK, but I still want them here. You, me and them. You say you have a zero-tolerance policy to bullying, you told me that you'll do whatever it takes to protect me. Now I need protection, I want justice to be seen to be done.'

She thought for a moment.

'OK. I don't normally give in so easily but you're the victim and I respect your wishes. I just hope this works.'

She picked up the phone on her desk and pressed a button.

'Mrs Franklin, can you bring Terry Stock and Alex Morris to my office, please.'

'And the girls,' I said. 'Priti Shah and Lola Muir.'

Mrs Martel continued, 'Mrs Franklin, could you also bring Priti Shah and Lola Muir?'

For a while we said nothing to each other. Mrs Martel sat down at her desk and began to look at some papers. I listened to the sound of pupils going to their lessons.

I wondered who would break the silence first. It wasn't me.

'Registration over, they shouldn't be long now.'

'It sounds like it,' I replied.

There was another long silence, then she spoke again.

'How's your mother?'

'She's doing well.'

'And have you seen Mrs Joseph lately?'

'Yes. She's fine. She's really into chess.'

'I didn't know that,' she said.

Just as she finished speaking there was a knock on the door.

'Come in,' said Mrs Martel.

Mrs Franklin opened the door just enough to put her head in and said, 'The four pupils you wanted to see are here.'

She opened the door fully and Terry walked in followed by the others. They lined up with me in front of her desk but I stepped away from them and put myself in between them and Mrs Martel. Mrs Martel sat back in her seat and folded her arms.

'Right. Why did you threaten and assault Jackson this morning?'

In perfect unison the two girls said, 'I didn't, miss.'

She started again. 'OK, boys. Why did *you* threaten and assault Jackson this morning?'

'Miss,' said Terry. 'You're always picking on us; he's not perfect you know. He keeps talking about us behind our backs.'

'I'm not always picking on you,' said Mrs Martel. 'There's four of you and there's one of him. Now answer my question. Why did you threaten him?'

'We didn't,' said Alex.

'You did,' I said.

'No we didn't,' he said again.

'Yes you did.'

'No we didn't.'

Mrs Martel had had enough. 'Yes you did, no we didn't, yes you did, no we didn't. You're acting like primary-school kids. I want to know what happened.'

I decided it was time to make my move.

'Actually, Mrs Martel, what they did to me is not that important. Why don't you ask them about the cider?'

'What cider?' she asked.

'Why don't you ask them?' I said, looking at them trying to hide their surprise at my question.

She turned to them. 'Have any of you been drinking cider in school?'

They all said, 'No.'

'That's right, miss,' I said. 'And I believe them, but ask them about the cider they used to get off Ramzi. Ask them about that.'

Alex and the girls held their heads down whilst Terry got more aggressive.

'He doesn't know what he's on about, miss, he's just jealous because everyone thinks he's a nerd; he's always making up stuff about people. He should get a life. Loser.'

Mrs Martel began to sound like she was getting angry. 'Now stop that and tell me about the cider.'

'I'll tell you about the cider,' I said to Mrs Martel. 'Ramzi and Lionel were different, so they used to gang up and bully them all the time, and then they started taking things off them, money and food, and watches, and it just got worse and worse.'

'He's taking rubbish, miss,' said Terry.

I turned to address them directly.

'It got so bad that you started getting cider from Ramzi, you made him bring bottles of cider to you a couple of times a week, and I know where he got that cider from. Do you? Well, let me tell you. He got it from the old lady you were throwing things at yesterday, the same lady who was in court saying she was Ramzi's mother. She longed for a son, so she struck up a friendship with Ramzi. Ramzi used to go and see her from time to time, but in the end she just used to buy cider for him, which you would take from him. Everyone knew that Ramzi and Lionel were weird, but you also knew they were weak, so you picked on them and made them serve you, and if I was weak you'd do the same to me.'

'He's talking crap, miss, he's losing it,' said Terry.

Then Alex put his foot right in it.

'They used to like bringing us stuff.'

'So,' said Mrs Martel. 'You admit that they used to bring you things?'

'I said stuff, not drink,' said Alex, trying to cover himself.

Now Terry was getting angry with Alex.

'Why don't you keep your big mouth shut? I told you to let me do all the talking.'

'You're not doing a very good job,' said Alex.

'Better than you, you stupid dunce,' Terry said, clenching his fist.

Lola's head shot up. 'Don't call him a dunce, you, who do you think you are?'

'Forget it, Lola,' said Priti.

'I won't.'

Their unity began to fall apart right in front of us.

'So,' said Mrs Martel. 'You were making Ramzi and Lionel get cider for you?'

'I'm not saying anything,' said Terry.

'Is anyone else saying anything?' asked Mrs Martel.

They all stayed silent. I walked to the door so their backs were to me. I signalled to Mrs Martel that she should meet me outside. She got the message.

'Wait one moment, I'll be right back,' she said.

On the other side of the door we whispered quickly. She started.

'What's going on here, Jackson?'

'Miss, they were really bullying Ramzi and Lionel, and that bullying was much worse than anything I'm getting. On the day of the stabbing something happened that I don't quite understand yet, but I am pretty sure that Ramzi and Lionel didn't bring a knife to school, and I know that one of them lot did.'

'Why do you think this?' she said, in a deadly quiet voice.

'Lionel's mum said she's never known him to take a knife to school and there definitely wasn't one missing from their house on that day. And Ramzi was stopped and searched by the police on the way to school; if he had a knife on him as big as the one that killed Mr Joseph it would have been spotted. And guess what? Martina Telford saw Terry and them with a knife on the day of the stabbing and when they saw me talking to her they began to get worried. That's why they started on me again this morning. They knew I was working on the case and they didn't want Martina Telford telling me what she saw.'

For the first time ever I saw Mrs Martel looking confused, and she was looking towards me for advice.

'I don't know what to think, and why are you so interested in this "case" as you call it.'

'Do you remember when I said I was having a kind of therapy? I said.

'Yes.'

'Well, this is my therapy.'

'So that's what you meant when you said you were having therapy that was individually tailored to you. Tell me more.'

'It's simple really. After seeing the stabbing I did

need therapy, but I didn't need to talk to a counsellor, I needed to understand what happened and why it happened, and I'm getting there – I think.'

She raised her eyebrows. 'I understand. So what shall I do now?'

'You have to trust me, Mrs Martel. I don't know exactly what happened the morning Mr Joseph was killed but there's more to it than we think. I'm getting very close to the truth, and I just know Terry Stock and his gang had something to do with it. Call the police, that's what you should do.'

Mrs Martel's voice got louder.

'I can't call the police. What do we say to them?

'Shh. I know they're going to crack, so it would be best if when they cracked the police were here. We could get them on underage drinking, we could get them on bullying, or if it helps I'd like to press charges on them for assault. But I know there's more.'

'No,' she said. 'I can't do it. I can't just call the police, we don't have a good enough reason.'

'You do, miss. They bullied me before and received a warning. They bullied me and hit me this morning. I want to charge them with assault. And that assault took place on these premises. I'm the victim here, are you going to support me?'

'You are the victim, and I'll support you, but are you sure you want to press charges, Jackson? Once the police are involved it's out of my hands.'

'I know,' I said. 'And I'm sure. I want to press charges.'

She walked off into Mrs Franklin's office. I heard her say, 'Call the police. Tell them to get here as quickly as they can.' She came back and muttered, 'I hope you're right, Jackson, but then again in some ways I don't.'

As we walked in the room we could see that we had interrupted a heated conversation.

'Right,' said Mrs Martel. 'I need to know about the cider. You were obviously forcing Ramzi and his friend to give you cider. Now tell me how often.'

They stayed silent.

She continued trying to get something from them.

'OK. How did it start? What did you do with all this cider? Did you pass it on to someone else? Did you sell it? Did you drink it? Come on now, have you suddenly lost your tongues?'

I looked at their faces. Alex was worried, Terry was looked grim and tense, Lola looked confused, and Priti was trying hard to hold back the tears. The moment she failed and I saw her wiping tears from her cheeks I knew I was winning.

Mrs Martel went over to look out of her window and said, 'Now I want to ask you all something, and I want you to think about the answer very carefully. On April the twenty-forth this year, why did you bring a knife into school?

Now Terry really shouted.

'Who said we brought a knife into school?' He pointed to me. 'Was it him? You're so dead, you are, you know that, don't you? You're dead.'

Priti started to cry aloud.

'And what are you crying for?' Terry shouted.

'Leave her alone,' said Alex.

Terry leaned over towards Alex and snarled, 'I told you to keep it shut. Why can't any of you lot listen to me?'

'Come on now,' said Mrs Martel. 'Tell me why you brought a knife to school, which one of you got the knife, and what happened to that knife.'

Then Alex cracked.

'Tell her, Terry, just tell her will you? I can't take it any more, she's gonna find out, just tell her and get it over with.'

Terry rocked forward and hit Alex with a punch that looked as if it went halfway round the room. Alex went down.

'How dare you!' screamed Mrs Martel.

'How dare I?' shouted Terry. He then proceeded to run around the room, kicking the furniture and throwing papers in the air. He went crazy, shouting like a boy possessed as he went on his rampage. 'How dare I? How dare I? I do what I want, no one tells me what to do, that's how dare I.'

The two girls ran into a corner, a lampshade just

missed Mrs Martel, who dived to the ground, Terry came and swung one of his wild punches at me but that missed and I dived to the ground.

Mrs Martel shouted, 'You'll not get away with this, the police are on their way.'

And as soon as he heard that he ran out of the door, knocking over Mrs Franklin, who had come to see what the noise was about. I ran after him. Through the corridors and out into the playground we went. Then I wondered what would happen if he stopped running. I couldn't fight him, but he outran me anyway. He went out of the school grounds and disappeared into the streets.

Alex, Priti and Lola were taken to the police station for questioning and Terry was easily caught by the police as he was trying to break into his own house. It didn't take long for all four of them to break down and speak up.

CHAPTER 29

My School Report

It was a tough case and it took me some time, but I got there in the end. Now let me break it down for you.

The day before the stabbing Terry and his gang ordered Ramzi and Lionel to bring them some cider but they were tired of it all and said no. Terry then told them that if they didn't bring the alcohol they would get beaten up even worse than before, but they still said no.

The next morning Terry brought a large knife to school in his bag; he was showing it off outside near a local newsagent's when Martina Telford saw them. All day they had been asking Ramzi and Lionel where the cider was but Ramzi and Lionel told them they hadn't brought any. Terry threatened to stab Ramzi and Lionel when classes were over. Terry's gang surrounded Ramzi and Lionel in an empty classroom and began to push them around. They were both slapped around their heads a couple of times then Terry pulled the knife. Alex, Lola and Priti ran away, which meant that Terry was outnumbered. The tables were turned and now Ramzi and Lionel managed to get the better of Terry and overpower him. Lionel now had the knife. This was where Lionel really went wrong. Instead of throwing the knife away or telling a teacher, he kept the knife to protect him and Ramzi just in case the gang came back, and they walked out to the playground. But the gang got back together and told Mr Joseph that they had just been threatened by Ramzi and Lionel. All Mr Joseph did when he caught up with them was touch Lionel on his shoulder, but Lionel was in such a state that he thought it was Terry and turned and stabbed him.

After all the abuse and hardship they had been through Ramzi and Lionel didn't really care that they had stabbed the wrong person. For them, in their state of mind, there was no wrong person. Things had got so bad that they wanted to be locked away, it would relieve them of the terrible lives they were living, so when the police suggested a sequence of events they didn't challenge them, they agreed with them. It all looked so straightforward, even for those of us who saw Mr Joseph go down.

I have learnt that you can see something happen right in front of you but still you are only seeing part of the picture. Nothing is as it seems. Seeing is not believing. Sometimes as well as seeing you have to feel, touch, experience, and use your intelligence, and even then you should still question. When I see people smiling now I don't presume they are happy. Ramzi and Lionel's lives were so different from each other's, but from everything I found out they were never happy. Can you imagine living for fifteen years unable to record any happiness in your life? They were constantly being called evil, but no one is born evil.

Terry Stock's gang were charged with underage drinking, perverting the course of justice, common assault, damaging property and possessing a dangerous weapon. The girls were both put on probation and Alex was given probation and twelve months' community service, and Terry got twelve months in youth custody to be followed by twelve months' probation. On the basis of the evidence I'd uncovered, Lionel and Ramzi were advised that they may be able to appeal against their convictions and hope to get reduced sentences at a retrial.

The good news is that the documentary was scrapped, I got pretty good exam grades, and I finished painting the front door.

The End

Now the headlines

How do you like your truth?
Gently spoken on breakfast TV
By a man and a woman who sit comfortably
Saying riots, and murder, when will it end?
As they struggle to act as if they are good friends.

How do you like your truth?
Bite-sized in sound bites cut easy to chew,
With a talking head saying the victim's like you,
And when you've digested the horrors you've seen
You find good, you find evil, with no in-between.

How do you like your truth?
Fantastic, sensational, printed in bold,
Today it's exclusive, tomorrow it's old,
All on the surface with nothing too deep
With a story about animals to help you to sleep.

How do you like your youth?
From perfect families with parents that care,
Or in perfect families but still in despair,
Ten out of ten parents say they'd not choose
To have bad kids like those kids they see in the news.

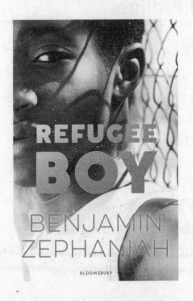
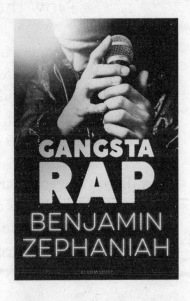
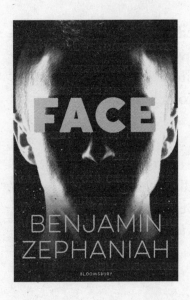